SECRETS AND SUSPENSE

A Clean Romantic Suspense

LORANA HOOPES

For the health care workers and virologists who have been fighting Covid-19.

When I finished Never Forget the Past last November, I began thinking about the idea for this book. I knew it was going to be about Cara and since she was former military, I began researching if the military studied viruses. At the time, I thought it would be interesting to write about an outbreak. Little did I know that Covid-19 would hit a few months later, and we would be living through our own outbreak. That actually made this book so much harder to write because I was so tired of being in quarantine.

Melioidosis, the virus discussed in this book, is a real disease that the military does study. I did take a few liberties in the infection timeline, but only because the timeline to show symptoms can be anywhere from two days to fifty-two years. As this is a suspense, the story needed to cover just a few weeks instead of years. The rest of the information about Melioidosis is actually true.

I hope that you enjoy this story and that wherever you are, you are staying safe and healthy.

❧ I ❧

CARA

Cara Hunter let the warm wind blow in the open window as she drove down the interstate in her red Ford Mustang. Her left hand drifted up to adjust her sunglasses, as her right tapped on the steering wheel, the rhythm close to the one blaring out of her radio. A smile played across her lips as she thought of seeing Steve again. She only came this way once a month, but it was her favorite day each month. Though she enjoyed running the bed and breakfast in Fire Beach, she missed working closely with Steve.

Perhaps it was the military regimen or the added sense of security that she missed the most, but Steve's dry sense of humor topped the list as well. Besides, doing the research on her own was not only lonely, but living the double life was beginning to take its toll on her. She'd noticed that in the mirror this morning as she got dressed. There were definitely more wrinkles around her eyes and a deeper crease in her forehead than there had been a year ago when she'd been forced to leave the base and create a secret identity in Fire Beach.

At first, she hadn't minded. It had been good to see Jordan again, and the bed and breakfast provided some relief from her other work. The work that consumed her nights and invaded her dreams. Even during the day, it kept her on edge. She had been forced to keep a tight circle of friends for fear of never knowing who she could trust, but she knew she could trust Steve. She could relax and be herself around him. These once a month visits were the only times she felt like she wasn't lying to everyone around her. The only time the tension truly melted from her shoulders even as they discussed mortality rates and vaccine issues. She just hoped he had found more than she had.

The last few weeks had been one setback after another. Of course, she wasn't dealing with the live virus strands or the rats - Steve had taken that on - but mapping the epitopes was no walk in the park either. It was just a little safer.

She slowed the car as she reached the turnoff for his street. Smiling, she wondered if he would have dressed today. He hadn't the last time she'd come, and she'd been shocked when he opened the door wearing SpongeBob pajama pants and an old Army shirt. He'd explained that since he'd left the base and rarely seemed to leave his house, he'd taken to only changing out of his pajamas for showers which she was almost certain had become fewer and farther between. He had always been eccentric, but the loneliness and stress had certainly taken a strange toll on him. She wondered what his neighbors thought of him.

As she parked the car a few spots from his door, a weird tingling sensation shot down her spine. On instinct, she turned the engine off and scanned the area looking for anything out of place and listening for any noise that didn't belong. Other than the silence that seemed thicker today than normal, nothing appeared contrary to how it usually was. Perhaps the stress was getting to her too.

She grabbed her laptop bag and headed toward his house. He'd picked a nondescript rambler in the middle of a residential neighborhood. "To blend in better," he'd said. She supposed it worked. Sometimes hiding in plain sight was better than hiding anywhere else.

After a final scan of the surrounding area, she knocked softly on Steve's door. "Steve, are you in here?" A feeling of unease washed over her as it creaked open. Steve never left his door unlocked. Like her, he was paranoid of being caught doing his research. Even though they'd been sanctioned by the military, what they were doing could be dangerous if it fell into the wrong hands. It was something she worried about every day, and she'd had enough conversations with Steve to know the fear had taken residence in his mind too.

She should turn around right now. Or call Jordan. At least if she had a detective with her, she wouldn't be blamed for whatever she might find inside, but she had to know. Careful not to touch anything more, she nudged the door open a little farther with her elbow.

The unease burgeoned into terror as she took in the room. Or what was left of it. Furniture had been shredded and lay upended across the room. Drawers hung like broken arms from the desk. Books and papers littered the floor, and an eerie silence filled the room. How she wished she had more than the small knife concealed in her boot.

The desire to call Steve's name again burned in her throat, but she clamped her jaws shut. Though it felt as if whoever had done this was gone, alerting them to her presence would be reckless if they were still in the house.

Instead, she took cautious steps around the mess, careful not to step on anything and leave footprints. As she did, she looked for any prints that might have been left by the perpetrator. It hadn't rained lately, so the chances were slim but even an indention on a piece of paper would help.

The living room opened to a kitchen which was equally messy. All the drawers had been emptied on the floor and the cabinet doors gaped open like hungry mouths. Someone had obviously been looking for something, and Cara knew they had probably found it.

Steve kept most of his research in a hidden closet in his bedroom, but if whoever had done this was this thorough, it was unlikely they hadn't found the room. She just hoped Steve hadn't been home when they had.

Exiting the kitchen, she proceeded carefully down the hallway. Steve's house was small - just a single bedroom after he and his wife had split up. That left only two more doors - the bathroom and the bedroom. Both doors were open, and Cara glanced quickly in the sparse bathroom before continuing to the bedroom.

Fear, rage, and disgust battled for her dominant emotion as she nudged the bedroom door open further and saw Steve lying face down on the bed. The puddle of brick-colored liquid surrounding him left no doubt that he was dead, and the open door to his secret closet at the other end of the room confirmed her suspicion that his research was gone.

There was no reason to stay any longer. She needed to get out of there before any of the neighbors saw her and tried to pin this murder on her.

Retracing her steps, Cara exited the house and climbed back in her car. The composure she had worked so hard to contain while in the house crumbled as her door shut. Tremors took over her body as she grappled with the knowledge. Someone had killed Steve. Was she next?

Her hand shook as she fumbled to get the key in the ignition. She needed to call Jordan and have him send someone to the scene, but first she needed to call Malone. She had to know if he knew and what he was going to do to protect her.

She punched in his personal number before throwing the car into reverse and backing away from the crime scene. Every nerve in her body wanted her to flee, press the gas and roar out of the area, but that would only draw unwanted attention. Attention she didn't need.

"Cara? What's going on?" The concern in Malone's deep voice resonated through her car, but it did nothing to calm her racing heart.

"Steve's dead." Choked with emotion, the strangled words hardly sounded like her voice.

"What?"

"He's dead. I stopped in for our monthly meetup, but I was too late. Someone beat me there. They trashed the place, killed Steve, and stole the research." Her hands gripped the steering wheel, the color in her knuckles fading to a dull white.

"Are you sure they got the research?"

Cara glanced down at her phone briefly as if glaring at it could send her ire to Malone. How could he sound so calm when she had just told him a member of their team was dead? And why did he appear more interested in the research than the man's life?

"Well, I didn't paw through everything and leave my fingerprints all over the place, but the house was trashed.

His secret room was open. I have no doubt they found everything they were looking for. Do you even care about Steve?"

Malone's sigh echoed through her speakers. "Of course I do, but I don't have to remind you Cara that our work is important. We're talking about saving lives."

"Right now we ought to be thinking about endangering lives. Steve had samples of the virus and mice that may or may not have been infected which means someone else now has them, and we have no idea what they plan to do with them. What if they come after me? Geez, Malone, how did they even know to come after Steve?" The questions tumbled out of her mouth like drips from a leaky faucet, but for each one she voiced, a dozen more scrambled for space in her brain.

"I don't know, Cara. I will look into it. For now, stay safe and see if you can get a breakthrough on that vaccine."

She wanted to ask him how exactly she was supposed to do that, but before she could say anything more, the click of him hanging up the phone reverberated through the car. She was on her own.

Well, not entirely on her own. She had Jordan and the rest of her friends in Fire Beach. They didn't know about her secret life, but she had no doubt they would help her out when she told them. She just had to make it back home.

2

COLE

Criminal Investigator Cole Davenport sighed as he looked around the most recent crime scene. To say it was a mess would be putting it mildly. Papers were scattered everywhere, drawers had been pulled out of desks and overturned, shredded pillows lay like flayed corpses leaving a trail of stuffing around the room. And of course, the body reposed in the middle of the mayhem. Face down with a massive wound to the head. "Is the head wound the cause of death?"

Wendy, the forensic technician, looked up at him and nodded. "It would appear so." Her gloved fingers examined the wound through the dark hair. "I would say blunt force trauma with a pointed object." She touched the skin of the body and moved one of the poor man's arms.

"Based on rigor mortis and algor mortis, I would say he's been dead eight to ten hours."

Cole nodded. Eight to ten hours would put the death in the middle of the night. At least that would explain the man still being in pajamas. Odd though. If he'd been sleeping, why attack with an object? Why not use a gun or smother him with one of the pillows? There were certainly enough of those around. Perhaps the man had woken to some noise? "Is there any sign of a struggle?" If he'd woken before he was hit, surely, he would have fought his attacker.

Wendy studied one hand and then the other before shaking her head. "I don't see anything that would lead me to make that determination, but we could scrape his nails to be sure."

"Please do." Cole bit the inside of his lip and studied the victim again. Something seemed off, but he was having trouble placing what it was. "Was he killed on the bed?"

Wendy pushed up her glasses with the back of her hand and looked around the room. "I doubt it. There's no spray in this room."

Yes, that was it. There was no splatter on the walls. If the man had been hit in the head, there would be a spray of blood. "Right." Cole scanned the room, noticing a door open at the back of the bedroom that he hadn't paid attention to before. He had assumed at first it was a closet, but now he saw that the closet was to his left. Nor was it a bathroom because that was in the hallway of this small one-bedroom house. So, why was there another door?

Careful to step around the mess to avoid contaminating any evidence, he made his way slowly to the open door. Stopping at the entrance, he pulled on his gloves and stepped inside. The room was small - perhaps it had been the closet at one time? Or had it been added after the fact? Whatever it was, it was clearly the place the attack had happened. Red droplets coated the wall like a sick abstract piece of art. So why move the body?

A shelf that had apparently functioned as a desk spanned one wall. It was devoid of anything now, but something told him it had once housed equipment of some kind. He ran his gloved hand across the surface and then held it closer to his face. What was that? Rice? A piece of grain? Removing a bag from his pocket, he dropped the speck inside to analyze later. Maybe the man ate in this room, but why? It certainly wasn't a cheery space. A solitary bulb hung from the ceiling casting a dim, eerie light on the room.

Underneath the shelf, he found a small fridge and a two-drawer file cabinet. Both were empty, but something inside him told him they hadn't been at one time. What had been the purpose of this room? It seemed too dark for an office. Some sort of research? But why keep it hidden? What exactly had he stumbled into?

Cole removed his gloves and ran a hand across the

back of his neck as he stepped out of the macabre room. "When you get done processing the body, can we process this room as well?"

Wendy looked up at him with an annoyed expression. "I'll do the whole room, Sir."

Of course she would. She was one of the best technicians in the department. Thorough to a T. "Thank you." There wasn't much more he could do here. He would have to wait for the evidence to come in and see where it led him.

3

CARA

Cara's thoughts were still on Steve's death as she pulled into her spot in front of the bed and breakfast. Jordan had agreed to call in the death, but his tone had been filled with questions. She knew she would have to tell him everything soon. He deserved that courtesy anyway.

Grabbing her laptop bag from the seat beside her, she locked the car and headed into the house. There was only one guest checked in currently, but it was nearing lunchtime and she needed to prepare something for her even if it was small.

After dropping her bag on the counter, she turned to the fridge to grab fixings for sandwiches. Mustard, cheese, meat. Her hand had just touched the plastic package when pain like she'd never felt before shot through her head and the world went dark.

A soft moan escaped Cara's mouth as she struggled to open her eyes.

"Cara, are you okay?"

She tried to fight the cloud fogging her brain, but it was hard. Her head pounded like an incessant drummer and everything felt fuzzy. Still, that had sounded like a man's voice - like Bubba's voice. What was he doing here? More importantly, why weren't her eyes cooperating as she tried to open them? Something had happened, but she couldn't quite remember what. It was there in the fog but just out of reach.

"This is Captain Makenna Drake of the Woodville police."

A female voice she didn't recognize cut through the foggy haze. Certainly not Bubba's voice. It was too high, but who was Makenna Drake? Not her guest. No, her guest was an artsy, elderly woman named Gladys here to walk the beach and look for sand dollars.

"I'm at Cara Hunter's bed and breakfast," the voice continued, "and she's been injured. Please send an ambo and a local unit to 212 Whistler Avenue."

"What happened here?" Confusion and concern collided in Bubba's voice.

"I have no idea."

And then like a curtain lifting before a play, the previous few minutes came back to Cara. Steve's death. Setting her bag down. Grabbing food for sandwiches, and something hitting her across the head. "I think I do. Can you help me up?" Cara's voice sounded strange and strangled in her head but at least the fog was dissipating. Unfortunately the clearing fog meant the throbbing pain in her head was increasing.

"I don't know if we should move her until the ambulance gets here." There was that feminine voice again.

"Nonsense." Cara forced her eyes open and immediately blinked against the blinding light. She struggled to sit up herself. "I took a hit to the head, but I'm fine."

Bubba's large hand gripped her arm, and he helped her to a sitting position so that her back leaned against the base of the bar. "You're still getting looked at, Cara."

"Fine, they can look at me, but I'll be okay." She touched the back of her head and grimaced at the bump she felt. She'd had worse, but this was definitely a good one. "I'm assuming there's no one still in the house?"

"We didn't see anyone." Bubba's cautious words were followed with a glance at the brunette next to him that told Cara they hadn't yet checked.

"But we didn't clear the house either. I'll do that now." As the woman stood, Cara finally placed who she was. Makenna Drake, the police officer from Woodville whom Bubba had called her about a few days ago.

"Do you know what happened?" Bubba's concerned

gaze returned to Cara as Makenna pulled her gun and stepped out of the kitchen.

"I know someone clocked me with something, but I didn't see them. I was getting lunch prepared for Gladys." Gladys! The woman's elderly face rose to her mind, and she tried to stand. "Is Gladys okay?"

Bubba pushed her back down. "Makenna and I will check on her. You are not to move until you get checked out. So, you have no idea who attacked you?"

Cara chewed on her bottom lip. She may not know who, but she could guess it was the same person who had attacked Steve. "They must have been quiet because I heard nothing." She could not believe that someone had gotten the jump on her. With her military background, that shouldn't have happened, especially after she saw what happened with Steve. Her radar should have been on heavy alert which meant not only had she been too distracted but it had to have been someone with experience. But then why leave her alive?

Her eyes widened as she remembered she had left her laptop on the counter. Oh no, had they gotten her research too? No, please God no. It would be bad if they had Steve's, but if they had hers too? She needed to check, but she couldn't right now. Not with Bubba and Makenna still here. None of them knew of her work, and for their protection, she needed to keep it that way.

"What's wrong?" Bubba must have noticed the change

in her expression because concern colored his normally deep, booming voice.

Cara thought quickly. She couldn't share the truth with him, but what could she say? "I was just thinking about Gladys. She's an elderly woman, and I would hate it if anything happened to her."

Bubba narrowed his eyes at her as if he didn't believe her. She couldn't blame him. That excuse had been lacking. "I promise Makenna will find out. You just need to rest and recover. Are you thinking it was a robbery?"

"Yeah, I mean I can't imagine what else it would be. I'll have to check the safe later and my room though to be sure."

Makenna returned at that moment but as her gun was back in her holster, Cara knew she had found nothing. "The rest of the place is clean. Your guest in room three was taking a nap and heard nothing, so that's a dead end too. I'm assuming the police will do a fingerprinting of the area when they arrive."

"That we will," Detective Jordan Graves said as he and his female partner, Al, stepped into the room. His eyes narrowed in concern when he caught Cara's gaze. "Are you okay?"

Cara had known Jordan longer than the others, and she could tell his worry ran deep from the creases in his forehead and around his eyes. The fact that he knew about Steve only deepened his concern, but the last thing she needed was Jordan sticking to her like glue. That would certainly make it hard to finish her mission. "I'm fine, Jordan. Someone got the jump on me, but it's just a little bump."

Disbelief flickered in his eyes as his hand ran across his stubbled face, but he knew her well enough to know she would tell him what she could when she got a chance. He would have questions for her later, especially coupled with this morning's call, but hopefully, he would save them until after she could check on her research and come up with a credible story.

"Okay, I love you guys, but can I get a little room to examine my patient here?" Ivy's soft feminine voice carried through the kitchen.

The group parted and Ivy squatted beside Cara. Her blonde hair was pulled back in a low ponytail today emphasizing the heart shape of her face. "How are you feeling?"

"I'm okay. Just a little dizzy."

Ivy flashed a light in Cara's eyes and checked her pulse. Then she checked the bump on the back of her head. "Well, there's a little blood back here, and since you were unconscious, I want to take you in for a head CT. It's probably nothing, but we don't mess around with head injuries."

Cara wanted to object - she needed to see how much the person had gotten - but she knew it was futile. With the group surrounding her, there was no way they were going to let her skip a hospital visit. She would just have to hope the doctor would release her soon and she could come back to check on her work.

"All right, fine. Bubba, I put Makenna in room five. The key is in the cabinet behind my desk."

"Don't worry, Cara, I'll help get her set up," Jordan offered. He knew the house almost as well as she did from all the times he had brought her someone to house and protect.

"I'll even have him give me a run down, so I can cover the place while you're gone." A smile accompanied Makenna's words, and Cara could see why Bubba had fallen for her. Not only was she pretty, but here she was offering to help out a total stranger.

"Thank you." Cara had never needed extra help. The B&B was never that busy, and she did most of her research in the early morning and late evenings, but suddenly she wished she had trained someone on how to run the business.

Makenna placed a hand on Cara's shoulder. "I'm happy to help. I was worried I might be a little bored without my regular police duties, but this will be a nice way to keep me busy when Bubba's at work."

The two exchanged a smile that made Cara's heart ache. Would she ever find someone who looked at her like that?

"And I'll get the crime lab out here to dust for finger-prints," Al said as she pulled her radio from her belt and stepped away.

"See? Everything is under control, so it's time to get you loaded up."

Ivy's smile was bright and encouraging, but Cara had a hard time returning it. If they knew what might be missing and what could happen if it fell into the wrong hands, they wouldn't be so glib. She just hoped that didn't happen.

❦ 4 ❧

COLE

Cole looked up at the knock on his door. Wendy offered a small smile as she tucked a strand of her dark hair behind her ear. He hadn't expected to hear from her so soon, but he had asked for a rush on the processing of the scene.

"I take it you have some information?"

"I do, though it doesn't make much sense, and I'm not sure you're going to like it." Her teeth bit down on her bottom lip, and she pushed her black-rimmed glasses up.

Cole rarely liked information he received on suspects. His job would be a lot easier if people didn't commit crimes, but seeing as how that would never happen, he had learned to accept that some suspects never made sense. It appeared this one would be another one of those.

"Liking it isn't my job. Looking into it is. What do you have?"

She stepped into his office and produced a manila folder she had been holding behind her back. "Well, I'm still processing a lot of the scene, but the item you found in that small room is a small grain. By itself, it makes little sense, but my examination also found signs that mice had been in that room."

"Mice?" Cole's brow furrowed as he leaned forward over his desk. "Like wild mice or pet mice?"

Wendy shook her head. "The piece of grain leads me to believe the mice were caged and fed, but beyond that I have no idea."

Cole shook his head as he tried to make sense of the information. This case was getting stranger by the moment. The victim had been in pajamas and killed in the early morning hours, but he hadn't been sleeping. Instead he'd been in a small secret room that housed mice, a mini fridge, and a file cabinet. What exactly had Steve Steele been up to? "Okay, that is strange, but I'm assuming from your face there is more."

She nodded and tapped her fingers against the folder. "After dusting the crime scene and the rest of the house, only one set of prints besides the owner's was found." She placed the folder on his desk and waited for him to open it.

He flipped it open to reveal the picture of a serious woman with short spiky blonde hair. "A woman?" It wasn't that women didn't commit murder, but that murder had been pretty brutal and most women didn't kill that way. They preferred poison or other more hands-free options.

"It's odd, right?" Wendy pushed her glasses up her nose again and folded her arms across her chest. "Hers were the only prints found and only on the front door. The rest of the house had been wiped clean. That usually indicates a professional, right?"

It did, but a professional wouldn't have left prints on the front door. So, was this woman a suspect or a victim? He turned the picture over to read what information they had about her, and his eyes widened. "She's ex-military?"

Wendy shrugged. "So it seems. Are you thinking rogue or some PTSD issue?"

"I don't know what I'm thinking right now other than the fact that you're right. This is definitely weird. However, it's also the only thing we have to go on, so I guess whoever Cara Hunter is, she's definitely a person of interest and someone I need to talk to as soon as possible."

COLE PULLED OVER AS SOON AS HE PASSED THE "WELCOME to Fire Beach" sign. He'd done some research about the place before he left his office, but he wanted to familiarize himself with Cara Hunter's information again.

Flipping open the manila folder, he tried to memorize her features. Slender, oval-shaped face, spiky blonde hair. A mole above her upper left lip and another near her right ear. Distinguishing features for sure. He turned the picture to peruse her information again. Formerly military, she now ran a bed and breakfast. Perfect. He would need a place to stay, and this would allow him the ability to observe her unnoticed.

After slipping the folder into his satchel, he put the car back in drive and continued into town. Though not a particularly small town, the downtown held the feel of such. Quaint shops lined both sides of the main street - restaurants, clothing stores, trinket shops, and more. Cole wondered if they actually saw many tourists pass through town, but maybe the beach drew them.

He followed the direction of his GPS as it told him to turn right on Whistler Ave. House 212 sat on the left, and while he knew it was the right place from the wooden sign outside, it could sure use a new coat of paint. The cheery yellow had faded to an almost soft cream color though it was weathered and peeling in places.

Cole parked his car and grabbed his satchel. The side-walk under his feet showed cracks and splits where plants had pushed their way through making him wonder if Cara bothered to do outside work on the house at all. Perhaps the bed and breakfast was just a cover? But for what? Weathered boards groaned beneath his feet as he stepped onto the porch while windchimes made from shells tinkled lazily in the breeze. Other than the slightly dilapidated exterior, the house exuded a relaxing beachy atmosphere.

He pressed the doorbell, hoping the interior was a little more cared for than the exterior. Footsteps sounded within, and a moment later, the door swung open, but the woman who stood on the other side was not Cara Hunter. At least not unless she had grown her hair out, colored it brown, and put on a few pounds. The woman staring back at him was not overweight, but she was definitely stockier than Cara's lean frame.

"Can I help you?" The woman's voice was friendly but hesitant, and her eyes studied him like only an officer of the law does.

For a moment, he was at a loss for words. He wanted to ask who this woman was and where Cara Hunter was, but that would necessitate a conversation about how he knew Cara, and he wasn't prepared to have that conversation with a stranger. Especially if he was right about her being in law enforcement. "Hi, I was hoping you had a room available to rent?"

Her eyes traveled the length of him before she nodded and stepped back, opening the door to allow him entrance. "Sure, follow me. Sorry about all this, but I'm not the owner. I'm just filling in for a bit."

"Oh?" He wanted to ask where she was, but he knew that would rouse suspicion. Had she not made it back from her killing spree yet? Or was it possible, she was a victim as well?

"I'm sure she'll be back soon though." Her brow furrowed as she stepped behind the front desk and stared at the computer. A momentary look of confusion clouded her face as she studied the screen. Either she was a new hire, or she was not a normal employee.

"So, how long will you be staying?" She tapped a few keys, smiling when she evidently found what she was looking for, and then stared expectantly at him.

How long was he staying? He wasn't sure. That depended a lot on who Cara Hunter was and whether she could help him find the killer he was looking for. "Um, I'm not sure how long my business will keep me here. A week? Maybe two?"

Her gaze narrowed at him, and he could feel her penetrating questions. Was she always this wary or was it because of whatever had happened with Cara?

"Okay, I don't know if she has any one coming in, but it looks open for now. I'll leave Cara a message to check in with you when she gets back. What kind of business are you in?" She asked the question lightly, but he did not miss the look in her eye as her gaze traveled over him again.

"I'm a contractor." That word was so vague, but it was one reason he loved it. He was a contractor - sort of. The department contracted him out often to help with other departments, sometimes even other states, but people rarely understood that in his line of work that was criminal investigation. Most of the time, people assumed he was a building contractor of some sort though he never felt he looked that part.

He adjusted the collar of his brown leather jacket and re-situated the satchel on his shoulder. Every fiber in him wanted to ask who this woman was, especially since it seemed she was as hard to read as he hoped he was.

"Oh. I'll put you in room one. If I can just get your signature here, I'll be happy to show you to your room." She clicked a button and smiled again when a printer behind her whirred to life. With a proud flourish, she rescued the paper and pushed it toward him.

After scanning the agreement to make sure there were no weird clauses or loopholes, he scribbled his name across the bottom, making sure it would be unreadable. He was no doctor, but he had spent time perfecting a messy signature. It was important in his line of work, and he certainly didn't need this woman looking into him before he knew which side she was on.

"Is that all you have?" Her eyebrow lifted as she pointed at the satchel on his shoulder.

"No, I have more in the car. I just thought I would get checked in first and make sure you had a room." He had a small suitcase in the car with clothes and toiletries, but the most important items he would need - his computer, his intel, and his gun - were all in his satchel and never far from his side.

The woman's tight-lipped smile displayed her disbelief, but she said nothing more as she grabbed a key and led the way down a hallway.

His eyes scanned the interior as he followed her, both to inspect it and to get a general feel for the layout. He would do a more thorough walk through later, but it was always good to know where his exits were.

The interior, while not his taste, was at least in better condition than the exterior. The walls were painted a light tan color, almost the color of sand, and beachy landscape pictures hung on the walls. Nothing seemed too personal, and he wondered if Cara kept that to her private area of the house or if she just didn't get a lot of personal items out.

Cole thought about Brian, the only other military person he'd known. He was the same way, and he'd informed Cole that it was for the protection of his family that he kept nothing personal at work. "You can never be certain of people's intentions, even the ones you know well," he'd said. Cole had thought it was a condition of the paranoia that sometimes surrounded Brian, but perhaps it was something taught in the military.

The woman opened the door to room one, pushed it open, and then stepped back. "Here you go. Breakfast is at seven, lunch at noon, and dinner at seven. The information to reach the front desk is by the phone in the room should you have any questions."

"Thank you. I'm sorry I never got your name?"

"It's Makenna. Captain Makenna Drake of the Woodville Police Department." With that she turned around and disappeared down the hallway.

A cop. Well, he'd been right about that at least, but why was the captain of the Woodville police here in Fire Beach? Were they also following up on Cara Hunter? Had she killed in another county as well? Or was this woman perhaps a friend of hers? So many questions fired in his mind, but they would have to wait until Cara Hunter returned. Cole entered the room and shut the door behind him. Now, his real work began.

CARA

Cara sighed as Nick stared at the computer screen, reviewing her charts. "Nick, I told you I'm fine. Can you please just sign the release forms so I can get out of here?" Cara had been in the emergency room department for six hours, and she was ready to get back to her house. She knew her laptop was gone - she had seen that much as Ivy loaded her onto the stretcher - but she had to know if they had found her other research. The research she kept hidden in a chest in her room.

Dr. Nick Pearson raised a brow and fixed her with a pointed stare. "Cara, you were hit in the head and passed out. Forgive me if I'd like to make sure you don't have lasting effects from a concussion."

Cara softened her tone, knowing that Nick was only doing his job, and her bristling tone would only delay her release. "And I thank you, but I'm not vomiting. I've been awake since I got here with no more dizziness. Other than a bump on the back of the head, I'll be fine."

He pushed back from the computer and stood. "I'm sure you will be, but one more check of your eyes and your head won't hurt anything right?" Grabbing a light from the wall, he flashed it in her eyes.

Cara blinked and stifled a sigh but allowed him to finish his exam.

After the exam, Nick walked to the small sink and washed his hands before turning back to face her. "Okay, I would feel better if you would stay a little longer, but I understand you have a business to run. Is there anyone there who can at least check in on you?"

The concern in his brown eyes was endearing though he was not Cara's type. "Actually, Bubba's girlfriend, Makenna Drake, is staying there. She's the police captain from Woodville."

Nick nodded and adjusted the stethoscope hanging around his neck. "That does make me feel better. Please have her check on you before you turn in for the night and first thing in the morning. If you do begin vomiting or having headaches, promise you'll come back in."

Cara doubted she would come back in, but she plastered on a smile and nodded. Truthfully, if her research had fallen into the wrong hands, she would have much more to worry about than vomiting and headaches anyway, but Nick didn't need to know that yet.

With her release papers in hand, Cara shot a text to Jordan as she let herself get wheeled to the front of the hospital. Calling Jordan came with risks, but he would be more suspicious if she didn't call him. Hopefully, she could convince him to drop her off and get back to his job. She would have a hard enough time avoiding Makenna; she didn't need to try to be ditching Jordan too.

The orderly dropped her off at the bench that sat outside the hospital, but Cara didn't have to wait long before Jordan pulled up.

"You get all cleared?" he asked as he walked around the car to open the passenger door for her.

Cara shrugged. "You know me. A little bump on the head isn't going to keep me down."

Jordan allowed her to slide into the passenger seat, but he held the door as she pulled to close it. "I do know you, and I know you have some pretty impressive defensive training. You want to tell me how this guy got the jump on you?"

That was a question Cara had asked herself many times over the last few hours. Whoever it was had to have been a professional, someone who knew how to enter quietly. But why would a professional leave her alive? "I guess I was distracted. I was still thinking about Steve, and I wasn't paying as close attention as I should have."

Jordan's jaw clenched as his eyes raked over her. He didn't believe her, but he couldn't prove she was lying either. "About that. Does your attack have something to do with your friend's death?"

She shrugged and picked at a piece of lint on her pants. "I don't see how it could since he lived in another county." Though she wanted to see his reaction, she was careful to keep her eyes from meeting his. She could hide behind her words, but he would see right through her if she looked at him.

"Hmm, one would think, but somehow, I think there's more to the story than that, Cara."

Cara shrugged. She might have to bring Jordan in, especially if her work was gone, but that time wasn't now. Not yet. Not until she knew for sure.

With a sigh, Jordan shut her door and returned to the driver's side. The short ride to her B&B was quiet but intense.

"Thanks for the ride," she said as she opened the door when he put the car in park.

Jordan's hand lifted to turn the keys in the ignition. "Let me walk you in."

"No need. I'm fine, and you still have work, right?" Cara not only needed to shake him, but she also needed to figure out who belonged to the strange car parked near her place. A guest? Or someone back to finish the job they'd started?

"Cara." The protest was evident in Jordan's tone, but she held up her hand to keep him from saying anything further.

"Look, Makenna is in there. She's law enforcement as well. I promise I will call you if anything further happens." She kept her tone short and terse, hoping he would take the hint.

Jordan looked as if he wanted to press the issue, but at that moment, his radio squawked, demanding his attention. Thankful for the intrusion, Cara took the chance to slip out of the car and head up the walk to her front door. Her eyes scanned the area for anything out of the ordinary as she approached as she had no desire to be taken by surprise again.

Everything appeared normal and calm, and her heart slowed slightly as she pushed open the front door. She didn't make it far before Makenna appeared, relief written all over her face.

"Oh, good, you're back. I've been trying to keep things running smoothly here, but this is not my forte, even with Jordan's crash training this morning."

Cara smiled. She knew that feeling only too well. She was a soldier and a researcher, so when they'd told her to open the bed and breakfast as a cover, she'd felt completely out of her element at first. However, it had soon grown on her, and she'd enjoyed meeting new people and helping out those in need. "I'm sure you did a wonderful job."

Makenna rolled her eyes and smiled. "Well, I did check a guest in. I put him in room one, but you might want to check that I did it right." Makenna led the way to the desk as if sure Cara would want to do this before anything else.

Another guest? Cara stifled a frustrated sigh. This house was about to be a little too full for her comfort. And her needed secrecy. "I'm sure you did a great job, but I'll look over it tomorrow. I'm still feeling a little tired, so I might retire early tonight."

Makenna nodded. "Of course. Sorry, I didn't mean to overwhelm you. I know I'm supposed to be a guest here, but please whatever you need, don't hesitate to ask."

If only she could, but what Cara needed was her work to be intact. She needed Steve to still be alive, and she needed her boss to care about his death. She needed to know who had Steve's work and what they planned to do with it, but none of that was anything Makenna could help with. "The doctor would like you to check on me in the morning to make sure I'm still alert, but other than that, I think I'm good."

"That sounds like a plan. I'll see you in the morning then."

As Makenna turned to go, Cara spoke up once more. "Thank you for all your help today, and I hope you get some time to enjoy Fire Beach."

Makenna offered a lopsided smile. "I'll try, but honestly I kind of enjoyed the action. Too much down time makes me nervous." She flashed a goodnight wave and disappeared down the hallway.

Cara chuckled softly as she watched Makenna walk away. She liked the woman. It was too bad they hadn't met under different circumstances because she was sure they would have been friends.

Pushing the thought away for now, Cara headed to her room. The moment of truth was upon her. She hoped she would find her research intact, but her gut told her it would be gone, and she would have to make the hardest decision of her life.

When she opened the door to her room, her heart sank. It looked as if a tornado had touched down inside it. Her bed was torn apart, and knife slashes gaped in her mattress. The drawers of her desk were up-ended on the floor, papers lying around like dead birds, but it was the sight of her trunk that seized her heart. The lock had been sawed off and it gaped at her, empty and accusing. Everything was gone.

❧ 6 ❧

COLE

Cole went down for breakfast bright and early the next morning, hoping to see Cara and ask her a few questions. She hadn't been around at dinner the night before, but he'd heard someone come in a few hours after. He supposed it could have been another guest, but it seemed unlikely as the town didn't appear to boast a booming nightlife. He'd spent last night researching the area and while it offered the beach and the touristy shops along the main street, there were only a few night clubs listed on the other end of town.

The dining area was bright and airy, reminding him of a poolside cabana. A beachy tan color covered the walls and each table sported a different vividly colored table-cloth. He chose the blue table this morning and sat down in the cushioned chair. A paper menu sat on the place setting, and after perusing it, he decided on the meat filled omelet.

"Good morning, you must be my new guest."

Cole looked up to find himself staring into Cara's eyes. Though bruised and puffy, he recognized her face from the picture he had spent hours memorizing. All the details were there, but the picture had not captured the beauty in her blue gray eyes or the definition in her cheekbones. He nodded. "I'm Cole, and you must be Cara."

The blink of surprise was the only indication he had caught her off guard. Even the hand holding the pot of coffee didn't shake an inch. She was good. Her head tilted slightly as her eyes perused his face. "I am Cara. Do I know you?"

"No, but I was recently acquainted with one of your friends." He watched for any twitch of her face, any tell that she knew what had happened to her coworker. Not a profiler by trade, he had studied enough of it to be aware of certain tells.

"Oh?" Her brow lifted slightly - the only hint of her curiosity. "Who do you mean exactly?" She kept her eyes down as she filled his mug but he knew she could see him in the corner of her vision.

Did he lay out all his cards right now or keep them close to his chest? Her appearance and demeanor suggested it was more likely she was another victim rather than a cold-blooded killer, so he might as well tip his hand. "Sergeant Steven Steele. That name ring a bell?"

This time he did catch her tense but only minutely. It appeared as a muscle twitch in her jaw and the slight color change in her knuckles as her grip tightened on the coffee pot. "I knew Steve. We worked together, but I haven't seen him in at least a year. Not since I retired from the military and opened up this place." She motioned with her free hand to the dining area as if that settled any issue.

So, she was adept at lying. He filed that information away for later use. Though his gut still said she was not his perp, the fact that the lie fell so freely from her lips gave him pause. He picked up his mug and studied her over the rim. "Hmm, that's quite interesting since your fingerprints were found on his doorknob."

He took a sip of the hot liquid as he watched the emotions flash across her face. The shock appeared first as her eyes widened to reveal more of the white. Disbelief followed next as her brows inched closer together creating a tiny crease in between them. Then, like a light switch, she shut them off, and her stoic demeanor reappeared. They had been so minor and occurred so quickly that he might have even missed them if he hadn't spent so much time watching people's expressions. Perhaps he should have become a profiler. A small seed of pride filled his gut followed immediately by the question of whether her shock came from his knowledge or from her getting caught?

"Who are you?" Her shoulders dropped as her brave exterior faltered. Pulling out another chair from the table, she sunk down into it.

He set the mug down and leaned forward. "My name is Cole Davenport. I'm a criminal investigator for Clarksville, Illinois. The better question is who are you Cara Hunter? Are you merely a person of interest in this case or are you a vicious killer?"

Her eyes flicked up to his, fire burning in their blue-gray depths. "You think I had something to do with his death?"

Cole leaned back, folded his arms across his chest, and studied her. "I think you know something about it. How much is what I'm not sure of yet."

She pushed back her chair. "Am I under arrest?"

The heat burning out of her eyes could have started a small fire, but Cole was determined not to let it phase him. "Not yet, but I'd certainly like to take you in for question-ing. We could do that here or I could haul you back to Clarksville."

Her eyes narrowed at him. "I may be a little rusty on police jurisdiction guidelines, but I would say you are out of line, Mr. Davenport, especially since you haven't witnessed me committing a crime, nor did you follow me here."

Dang, she was good. And pretty when she was angry. Heck, she was pretty anyway, but something changed in her face when she was annoyed. It became sharper, more angular, making her look like a Greek goddess carved from stone. Cole unfolded his arms and leaned forward again. "While you might be right about that, I could certainly pick up the phone and ask an officer of Fire Beach to bring you in for questioning. I'm sure they would be happy to cooperate if they knew it involved a murder."

She had not expected those words; he could tell from the clenching of her jaw. "You do that. In fact, why don't you ask for Detective Jordan Graves? Not only is he a friend of mine, but I called him when I found out about Steve. He's the one who called the murder in to your department, and I'm sure he'd be happy to help you out. I'll get your breakfast, but then you'll be needing to find a new place to stay. I'm sure you understand."

The corners of Cole's mouth twitched. Tough and pretty. He couldn't remember the last time he had met a woman who interested him so much. Why did she have to be a suspect? "Of course. I'll have the meat omelet by the way." He held her gaze as he handed her the paper menu.

She snatched it from his hand before executing a perfect pivot and disappearing into the kitchen. He realized as she walked away that he probably should have waited until he had his food to spill his cards. He'd heard enough stories of cooks and waiters spitting in people's food before bringing it out that he should have known better than to poke a bear, but he just couldn't help it. Cara excited him, and he had enjoyed verbally sparring with her. More than he had with anyone in a long time, and though he hoped she didn't spit in his food, he wasn't sure he would have acted differently had he thought the situation through.

A slight chuckle escaped his mouth as he played back the scene in his mind. He wondered if her tough exterior came from the military or farther back? Though he knew he shouldn't be interested in her, especially since she was still his number one suspect at the moment, he couldn't help pondering the jigsaw puzzle that was Cara Hunter.

Ten minutes later, his food came out, but it was brought by the woman he had met last night and not Cara. Her face held no trace of friendliness.

"You want to tell me who you really are and why you're here?" She set the plate down hard enough to cause the utensils to jump. Angry daggers laced her carefully chosen words.

He motioned to the chair across from him, inviting her to sit. "You first."

Narrowing her gaze at him, she pulled out the chair and sat down. "I already told you who I am. Makenna Drake of the Woodville police department."

Cole picked up the salt shaker and pointed it at her before sprinkling a few of the white cubes on his eggs. "Why is a member of the Woodville police department here?"

She leaned back in her chair and pursed her lips as if debating whether to answer his question or pose one of her own. "I'm not here on business. I came to see if I wanted to move to Fire Beach. Your turn. What are you doing here?"

"I'm a criminal investigator in Clarksville. Yesterday, I walked through a pretty horrific crime scene. I'm here because the only prints found in the place besides the owner's belonged to one Cara Hunter."

Makenna leaned forward, placing her arms on the table. "I'm sure I don't have to tell you that you have no jurisdiction here. Did you even alert the Fire Beach police you were coming?"

"No, because I wasn't planning on arresting her. At least not yet." He speared a bite of omelet and pointed the fork at Makenna. "She's a person of interest at the moment." Also an interesting person but that was beside the point. "Look, either she's the woman I'm looking for or someone is probably looking for her. Neither option bodes well, and considering her appearance, I would wager that someone already came looking for her but didn't finish the job. I'm also here to make sure they don't." He placed the speared egg in his mouth.

"I see. Well, I don't know this town well, but from what I've heard, they stick together. I'd be careful who you go poking around here." Having said her piece, she pushed back from the table and headed back into the kitchen.

Cole committed her words to memory as she walked away.

7

CARA

Cara leaned against the counter and ran a hand across her forehead. What was she going to do? Malone had told her to keep working, but not only was some of her research gone - she had backed up a lot of it to the cloud but not everything - she also didn't have her laptop. And now she had a criminal investigator on her tail. How was she supposed to keep working and keep what she was working on a secret? Not only that but Jordan was sure to have questions after yesterday, and if Cole called the police on her, he would have to bring her in. This was a mess.

Top that off with the fact that someone now had access to a deadly virus and it was turning out to be a bad day indeed. If only she knew who was behind the murder and the theft or what they planned to do with the virus. Did they have enough to infect people? And if they did, what was their plan? Did people here need to worry?

"You want me to run his name? See if he's telling the truth?" Makenna asked, entering the kitchen.

Cara barely knew the woman, but she had been a godsend already. She'd watched the bed and breakfast yesterday while Cara was still in the hospital and she'd offered to help out with breakfast while Cara composed herself. If she did this much for strangers, Cara definitely wanted her as a friend. "No, I don't know why, but I think he's telling the truth."

Makenna's lips folded into a tight line. "Were you at the crime scene?"

Cara's eyes shot to her. "How did you-"

She pointed toward the dining room with a nod of her head. "Your friend out there told me that's why he's here. Said your prints were the only ones there. So, is he telling the truth about that?"

A deep sigh shook Cara's shoulders, and her hand scratched at the back of her neck. "I was, but it's not what you're thinking. I didn't kill Steve. In fact, as soon as I realized he was dead, I left his house and called Jordan."

"And who was this Steve? Friend? Boyfriend?"

Cara shook her head. "Nothing like that." She pushed off the counter and walked a few feet away from Makenna. Makenna was a cop, but could Cara trust her? She stifled another sigh as she realized it didn't matter. One way or another, her work here was going to get discovered. She might as well tell the story herself.

"He was sort of a friend. We worked together."

"Worked together?" The confusion was evident in Makenna's voice and echoed in the furrowed lines of her brow.

A soft chuff escaped Cara's mouth as she turned to face Makenna. "How much did Bubba tell you about me?"

Makenna shrugged. "Not much. He said you were former military and now you owned the bed and breakfast. Evidently, you're pretty handy to have around when people are in trouble, but that's all. Why?"

Cara chewed on the inside of her lip as she thought about how to tell her story. "Most of that is true only I didn't leave the military."

The furrow on Makenna's brow deepened, and she folded her arms across her chest. "What do you mean? Were you never in the military?"

Cara shook her head. "No, I definitely was. I mean I never left because I'm still in."

"I don't understand. There's no military base around here, is there?"

"No. There isn't. I was sent here undercover. Steve was sent to Clarksville."

Makenna's eyes widened as the pieces clicked into place. "The break in?"

"Yeah." Cara ran a hand through her short hair. "I don't

know why they didn't kill me too, but whoever killed Steve took everything he had been working on. All my research is gone as well."

A fire of determination flashed in Makenna's eyes. "What can I do to help?"

"Makenna, I can't ask you to do that. You're supposed to be spending time with Bubba and seeing if you like it here, not getting sucked up into my drama."

Makenna offered a slight smile. "If I decide to stay here, then your drama would be my drama too. Besides, if I know Bubba, he'll want to be in on this as well. As will your friend Jordan, I'm sure."

Cara returned the grin. "You know for someone who just got here, you seem to know a lot."

"It comes from years of being a police officer. I didn't make Captain by sitting on my thumbs. Now, what do we need to do?"

"We need to get everyone together and share what information I have. The police department and the hospitals need to know what to be looking for in case attacking Fire Beach is the plan. I certainly hope it's not, but it's better to be prepared."

Makenna jerked her head toward the dining room. "What about our friend out there? Do we bring him in?"

Cara hesitated. She didn't know Cole Davenport from Adam, but he'd made it clear he wasn't letting this go. She just wasn't sure if he was a friend or a foe. However, the old adage popped into her mind - keep your friends close and your enemies closer. Whatever he was, keeping him close seemed to be the best answer. "Might as well. Maybe he can be of some help though I'm not sure how."

"We'll figure it out." An audible internal rumbling broke the silence and Makenna placed a hand on her stomach. "Can it wait until after breakfast though? My stomach is telling me it's time to eat."

Cara smiled. "I think we have time for that. What can I make you?"

"How about a meat omelet with cheese and sourdough toast?"

"Perfect, I'll bring it right out."

As Makenna left the kitchen, Cara issued a sigh. She had no idea how she was going to fix this, but her own stomach had begun protesting as well. Might as well feed it while she played the scenarios over in her head.

Grabbing the eggs from the fridge, she whipped up Makenna's omelet and one for herself and headed out to the dining room. After giving Makenna her breakfast, she pulled out the chair at Cole's table again and sat down across from him. "It appears you and I need to talk. In private."

Though he did not smile, there was a knowing twinkle in his eyes as if he'd known this was coming. It drove Cara crazy and sent her heart fluttering in her chest. She didn't like the fact that he affected her - she prided herself on the ability to avoid being sucked into the charms of handsome men - but something about him called to her.

"I figured you'd start to see it my way."

He took a sip of his coffee, and Cara had to force her eyes away from his lips. Ugh, why did he have to be so good looking? "So, how long have you been a criminal investigator?" Perhaps if she lightened the mood for a minute, she could focus on her breakfast and not how soulful his eyes were.

"A few years now. I almost joined the military like my dad but just couldn't stomach it."

"Too patriotic for you?" Cara asked as she speared a chunk of omelet.

"No, too strict. I like being my own boss. Never been good at following other people's orders. Probably another reason I became a CI instead of staying on the regular police force."

Cara could appreciate that. Though she enjoyed serving, she had also enjoyed being her own boss this last year. "And you enjoy it?"

Cole opened his mouth to speak and then closed it. He took a sip of his coffee and stared into his mug for a minute before meeting her gaze again. "I did for a while. It filled a hole, but now," he shook his head. "I don't know. I feel like it might be time to do something else."

Cara wasn't sure why, but his words saddened her. Something from his past haunted him, but that was true of nearly everyone. She certainly had some ghosts in her past she wished would stay out of her mind. They finished the rest of their breakfast in silence, and when her plate was empty, she pushed her chair back and grabbed both of their plates. "If you want to follow me into the kitchen, we can talk after I drop these off."

Cole downed the last of his coffee and joined her. Cara could feel Makenna watching them, but she refused to turn around and meet the woman's gaze. She had no answers yet for the silent questions she knew would reside there.

When the kitchen door closed behind them, Cara placed the dishes in the sink and then turned to Cole. "I'll tell you what I know, but I want some answers first."

He shoved his hands into the pockets of his brown leather jacket and leaned against the fridge. "I think I've answered enough of your questions. It's my turn."

Cara shrugged. She was honestly surprised he had answered as many of her questions as he had.

"How did you know Sergeant Steven Steele?"

"We worked together. I wasn't lying about that."

His brow lifted, and his eyes stared so intently into hers that she almost felt he was boring a hole into her soul. "But?"

Cara bit her lip. Her gut said she could trust Cole, but what if he was behind this? What if the man in front of her wasn't the real Cole Davenport but the man who had attacked her back to finish the job? "Do you have ID?"

"What?" The question had obviously caught Cole off guard.

"ID. You said you're a criminal investigator named Cole Davenport, but I don't know what Cole Davenport looks like. If you are him, you won't mind showing me ID." She folded her hands across her chest and fixed him with her most intimidating stare.

The corners of Cole's lips twitched as if he was fighting a grin. "You are exactly as I imagined you'd be."

She wasn't sure what he meant by that though she guessed he had dug up some information on her when her fingerprints had crossed his system. Still the thought of him imagining her in any way sent a heat crawling up her neck.

Cole pulled his wallet from his pocket and handed it to her. Flipping open the dark leather flap, she found herself staring at a less than flattering but very similar image of the man in front of her. "Not your best day, I see." She couldn't help the teasing jab and enjoyed the pink that graced his handsome features as he reached for the wallet back.

"It was early in the morning and a long day at the DMV." He shoved the wallet back in his pocket. "Now, you want to answer my questions?"

This was it. She was going to take a leap of faith and trust a man she barely knew. "Steve and I were tasked to study a virus that was infecting troops when they went overseas. I was there, but I didn't kill him."

"What were you there for then?"

"We met up once a month to compare our findings and share information." Her right hand roved up and down her left arm. "I didn't know he was dead until I got there. I touched the door, but when it swung open, I knew something was wrong. Careful not to touch anything more, I walked through the place to check on Steve. When I saw him on the bed and the door to his secret closet open, I left. I knew that if they had gotten to him, I was bound to be next."

She took a deep breath in an effort to calm her jittering heart. "It was wrong to leave the scene, but I was trying to protect the research. Not that it mattered. The first thing I did was call my boss to let him know. Then I dialed Jordan and asked him to call it in. You can check with him."

The muscles in Cole's throat jumped as he held Cara's gaze. "And when were you attacked?"

"As soon as I got home. I had a guest and got back in time to make lunch. Whoever it was attacked me while I was getting ingredients out of the fridge. I don't know why they didn't kill me too. Maybe they meant to but Bubba and Makenna arriving threw them off their game. I don't really know how long I was out before they arrived." She shrugged and shook her head. "Or maybe there's another reason. Until I know who did it, I don't really have an answer for you."

Cole nodded and resumed his leaning stance against the fridge. "Fair enough. How about you tell me about this virus study then."

Cara took a deep breath. This was a much longer story. "I joined the military right out of college. Unlike you, I enjoyed the direction and the rigor. While I was in, it became apparent that I had a knack for research and my name was passed on to key people higher up the ranks. A few years ago, I was brought into a special group working on a vaccine for Melioidosis."

Cole shook his head. "I'm not familiar with it."

"Most people aren't." Cara stepped away from the sink and began pacing. She couldn't tell this story standing still. Not when every nerve in her body was on edge. "It's not a disease that we hear about much in the United States. It's typically found in Southeast Asia and Australia, but it infects a lot of troops who deploy to those places. Because of this, the military wanted to study it and try to find a vaccine that could prevent its transmission."

"That sounds logical, but I'm assuming something bad happened."

Cara nodded thinking back to the day everything had changed. "Yeah, about a year ago, our boss told us that we needed to take a different part of the research and split up. Evidently, he had been informed there was a mole in the unit who was trying to steal our information. The hope was that if we took separate pieces then even if something happened to one of us, the information wouldn't fall into the wrong hands. Unfortunately, not only did the killer steal Steve's research and the virus samples, but-"

"Yours? Did they get it before they attacked you?"

She ran a hand through her hair. "Or after. I'm not sure, but my laptop was gone and when I got back from the hospital yesterday, I went to my room to check. The room had been trashed and all of it was gone."

A low whistle escaped from Cole's lips. "What does this mean?"

Cara shook her head, wishing she had those answers. "I'm not sure, but the one thing I do know is that I have to start over. I'll need a new computer, but I backed up some of my work and some of the information I had gotten from Steve to a server in the cloud. It's not enough, but I need to access it to try and figure out what they might try to do with it, and I need to make sure we have the medication to treat it at the hospitals. I have no idea if they plan to unleash it here or somewhere else, but I want to be prepared just in case."

Cole chewed on his bottom lip as he digested her information. His hand raked across his stubbled chin, sending a soft scratching noise through the stillness that sent a tremor down her spine. "Okay, while I'm sure you understand that

I still need to do my duty in investigating Steve's death, I'll help you however I can."

His words sent a shiver of excitement down her spine. This was no time to be falling for a man, but she couldn't deny that working with him appealed to her on more levels than one. "I'm sure I don't have to tell you that this could be dangerous."

He held her gaze as if accepting the challenge. "I'm sure I don't have to tell you that doesn't matter. I have a job to do, and I'm not going anywhere until it's done."

"Good. Well the first thing we need to do is get everyone together. I'd rather only repeat this information once."

CARA STARED OUT AT THE SMALL GROUP SHE HAD assembled and tried to gather her courage. It was one thing to tell Cole and Makenna whom she didn't know well, but now she was going to have to tell her closest friends that she'd been lying to them for over a year.

"Thank you all for coming. I know you have places you'd probably rather be."

"Just maybe eating at Fire Dreams," Bubba piped up. "Is there a reason we couldn't have this discussion there?"

"Actually there is. I didn't want to create a panic."

"A panic over what exactly?" Jordan asked as he leaned forward.

"For the last year I've been working undercover on a vaccine for the military." Though eyebrows raised and eyes widened, no one interrupted her, so Cara took a breath and continued. "Due to a suspected mole in our organization, my fellow researcher and I were separated and each sent with a part to study. We kept in touch through secure channels when we had to share information and met once a month in person, but most of it was on our own. A few days ago, the other member of my team was murdered. You may not have met Cole Davenport yet, but he is a Criminal Investigator in Clarksville where my coworker was killed."

"And how does this involve us?" Dr. Nick Pearson asked. Cara had made sure he and his fellow doctor, Brady Cavanaugh, were both in attendance. She hoped they would share her information with the rest of the hospital.

"That's the main issue. I don't know." She looked to Cole. "We don't know. There's a chance that whoever took this information plans to infect people with Melioidosis. It's a pretty terrible disease if not treated. With no treatment, nine out of ten patients die. With treatment that drops to four out of ten."

"That's still terrible statistics," Brady said, and Nick nodded in agreement. "What is the treatment?"

Cara turned to the easel which held a large pad of

white paper. She had scribbled a few things down she thought would be helpful before calling the meeting. Flipping the first page up, she said, "There are a few options. Ceftazidime and Meropenem are the most common. Both can be administered through an IV. There are also a few oral options, and I'll be sure to get that information to you both. So, we need to make sure we have the treatments on hand and if not, we need to get them."

Brady and Nick exchanged glances and began taking notes in their phones.

"Okay, so let's assume infecting people is their plan," Ivy said softly from her position with the rest of the firefighters, "what am I looking for when I go out on a call? And how contagious is it?"

Cara nodded and flipped the current page up. "As you can see, it can present in lots of different ways. It could present as a localized infection in which case you would see pain, swelling, fever, ulceration, or abscess. It could also present as a pulmonary infection with a cough, chest pain, high fever, headaches, or anorexia. If it gets into the bloodstream, you could expect to see fever, headaches, respiratory distress, abdominal or joint pain, or disorientation. Finally, it could also be a disseminated infection. The symptoms of that are fever, weight loss, stomach or chest pain, muscle or joint pain, headaches, or seizures."

She paused to take stock of the room. Though most were following her, a few glazed eyes stared back at her.

She needed to put it in plainer terms. "Needless to say, that's a lot of symptoms, but fever, cough, headache, and pain are the big ones. I know that leaves it pretty open because a lot of things can present with those symptoms, but my hope is that we'll keep our eyes open and take a second look at anything that might be suspect. Anything that looks like pneumonia, flu, or tuberculosis should definitely be checked. As for contagion, again it depends. It's not generally transmitted from person to person."

"Well, that's good news," Bubba said.

"Yes and no." Cara wished she had more definitive answers for her friends. "It is generally transmitted through contaminated soil, water, or air particles."

Silence fell around the room as everyone processed what that meant. "So, you're saying if they put this in the water supply or find a way to disperse it in the air, it would infect a lot of people?" Makenna's voice held the serious tone that Cara saw displayed on every face around the room.

"Unfortunately, that's exactly what I'm saying. It's possibility as a weapon of bioterrorism is one reason that we were studying it. The military wanted to be ahead on a vaccine in case this ever happened. I don't want to scare the public yet which is why I'm not holding a press conference, but if we see a case, I'll have my boss notify the CDC. I don't think they'll come until we have an active case anyway, but there's one more thing we need to consider."

Jordan caught her eye, and she could tell from his gaze that he knew the issue. "If they find a way to mutate it, none of this will matter, will it?"

"Probably not," Cara said. "The good news is that mutating a virus is hard, but there's always the chance it mutates on its own which is why we all need to be vigilant. We need to keep our eyes open for anyone acting suspiciously and especially for any cases that come in. We need to know how they got infected."

"And what about the military?" Jack Stone asked in his deep, gravelly voice. As head of the Special Investigations Unit, Cara had decided he had to be involved though he was the only man in the room who actually intimidated her. His name fit him to a T as she had rarely seen a smile break through his stony exterior.

"I'll be continuing to work on a vaccine. Perhaps my boss can send some other researchers to help, but we weren't that close before now, so I'm not as hopeful on that front. Of course, I'm sure he will be trying to find out who took the research as well. Finding that out will help us determine their next moves." Cara paused as she stared out at the people that she called friends. "I know this is a shock and not what we want to hear but thank you all for coming."

8

COLE

Cole still wasn't sure how to feel about Cara. His gut told him she was a victim, especially after listening to her tell her friends the truth. That couldn't have been easy, and while they had stuck by her, promising to help in any way they could, Cole had felt the tension in the room. It permeated the air, remaining even after the last person had left.

"Where are we going?" he asked as he quickened his pace to keep up with Cara. Though she was shorter than he was, she took long strides and covered distances quickly.

"Fire Dreams. It's Jordan's restaurant. I don't know about you, but I needed to get out of the bed and breakfast for a bit." She stopped and turned to face him. "Besides, they have great food."

His stomach rumbled at the mention of food. He didn't

think he had eaten since breakfast. The day had been a whirlwind after that with Cara showing him her trashed room and then the discussion with her friends.

She pulled open the doors to the restaurant, a casual place with a homey feel. The lowered lighting invited intimate conversations and the color palette appealed to the eyes.

"Hi, Cara," the hostess behind the podium said as Cara approached. "Two today?" A wide, sincere smile lit up her face as she grabbed two menus.

Cara nodded before addressing the woman. "Hi, Ginny. How're you doing?" She obviously knew the woman, and Cole wondered again how close knit this community was.

"Pretty good now that life has calmed down," the woman said, stepping out from behind the podium.

"You seem to be settling in well," Cara said as Ginny led them to a table.

The woman's smile grew even larger as she stopped at a table. "I am. Graham and Jordan have been amazing bosses, and I can't thank you enough for helping me out when I first got here."

"It's what I do," Cara turned her attention to Cole, "and I am always happy to help."

The hostess looked between them for a minute as if sensing the tension. Then she handed them each a menu. "Well, thank you. Here are your menus and your server should be with you shortly."

"Is there anybody in this town you don't know?" Cole asked when the hostess was out of earshot.

"Of course, the town isn't that small."

No, it wasn't. While it had a small-town feel, the town was rather large which prompted him to ask the question that was on his mind. "I know this is all a guess, but what do you think the odds are that Fire Beach is the target?"

Her smile faded as his words hit home. "Honestly, I doubt it. Although it's possible something gets released here, I fear there is something much bigger and more nefarious underfoot. Fire Beach is a nice place, but we have nothing political to be gained here."

"Unless it's personal." Cole hoped it wasn't. He was beginning to like Cara, and as much as he wasn't sure he liked the feelings he was having towards her, he didn't want her to be the bad guy. Nor did he want anything to happen to her or her friends.

"Let's talk about something else, shall we?" Cara switched the topic as she opened her menu. "You said this might be your last job, but you look too young to retire. What do you plan to do next?"

That was a very good question and one which Cole didn't have an answer for. He honestly didn't even know for sure this would be his last job. What he did know was that, for the first time in years, he was lonely and tired of it. The fact that he was a criminal investigator made it hard enough to find a woman who wasn't afraid he would use his skills on her, but add to that his time away from home and keeping a relationship was impossible. Or at least it had been the few times he had tried it after... No, he wasn't letting his mind go there.

"To be honest? I have no idea. I guess I'd just like a job where I could be home more than I am. Living out of hotels is only fun for so long." He held her gaze for a moment before dropping his eyes to the menu. It had been a while since a woman had affected him the way Cara did, and he wasn't quite sure how to handle the emotions coursing through him.

"I can understand that. I enjoyed moving around with the military at first, but I've come to appreciate having a place to call home."

He caught the subtle hint of sadness in her voice. "Will you have to go back to active duty when this is over?"

Cara bit her lip and shook her head. "I don't know. I only have a few more months before I'd need to re-enlist. I had planned on it because I couldn't imagine leaving the project unfinished, but now? I'm not so sure."

The waitress approached then and took their order. They ate in silence when the food came, but Cole could feel the tension still lingering between them. "What's your next move?"

Cara blinked at the sudden question and swallowed her food before answering. "Um, a call to my boss I guess, to see if he can spare some other researchers, and I need to purchase a new laptop. I can't do much until I have that. Then I'd like to follow up with the hospital to make sure they have the medicine."

It wasn't a detailed plan, but Cole wasn't sure they could get more specific until they knew more. "Well, I'm not sure what help I can be, but whatever you need, you let me know."

Her eyebrow lifted. "You're staying then? Even though I'm not Steve's killer?"

Did she want him to leave or did he hear a note of relief in her voice? "I figure whoever attacked Steve and then you may still be in the area. Until I know for sure, I think it's best that I stay close. Besides, I have no other clues yet. My lab tech will call if she finds anything else out, but for now? My best chance of catching Steve's killer is helping you."

He meant the words, but he also didn't mind the fact that his lack of clues gave him an excuse to remain near Cara.

9

CARA

Cara picked up the phone and dialed Malone's number. After their meal at Fire Dreams, Cole had gone with her to purchase a new laptop, and now that it was up and running and she had downloaded both her and Steve's most recent research, getting Malone's help was the next step. She hoped that he could spare some help.

She hadn't been close to finding a vaccine on her end, and neither had Steve unless he'd found something in the last month. Without his help, it would take her even longer to find a vaccine and with the looming possibility of an exposure, that was time she didn't have.

"This is Malone."

"It's Cara."

"Cara? Are you okay?" It had been fewer than forty-eight hours since she'd last spoken to him, but the concern in his voice made it seem as if it had been weeks.

That was certainly a loaded question considering what she'd been through in the last two days. "I've been better. Someone attacked me when I got back to my place yesterday morning. I fared better than Steve, but all of my research is gone as well."

"So, whoever did this now has both of your research?"

"I'm afraid so. I was able to get a new laptop, and Steve and I had both uploaded most of our research to a cloud server. I haven't checked to see if he had discovered anything new yet, but I was wondering if you could send anyone to help. I have friends here, but none of them are researchers."

There was a long pause on the other end. Long enough that Cara held her cell phone out to make sure she hadn't lost the call. "I'm not sure. It's been a little busy here, and we're short staffed already."

Was he serious? She knew the department was small, but was there really no one he could spare? Had he forgotten how serious Melioidosis was? "What if they unleash it here?"

Malone sighed. "I understand your concern, Cara. Somehow, I doubt Fire Beach would be the target of an attack, but I'll see what I can do. Give me a few days."

"Fine." Disgusted, Cara ended the call. She had hoped

Malone would be available to help, but it appeared she was firmly on her own.

"No luck?" Cole stared at her, sympathy oozing from his gaze.

Cara shook her head. "Not much. Malone said the department is short staffed, so he isn't sure he can send someone. Of course, he also believes Fire Beach isn't the target, so that probably explains his nonchalance. Regardless, one would think he would want a vaccine found for this virus sooner rather than later. Especially now that someone has our research."

Cole stood from the chair he had been sitting in and crossed to Cara. "What can I do to help?"

She issued a sarcastic chuckle and leaned against the fireplace mantle. "Can you map an epitope or run an antigen test?"

Confusion clouded Cole's face, and he shook his head. "I'm not even sure what you just said qualifies as English."

"Now you see my problem. Fire Beach isn't exactly teeming with medical researchers and most of what I read would be Greek to everyone else."

"Fair enough. You might be the only researcher here, but you seem knowledgeable. I have no doubt you can get the job done."

His eyes locked with hers and Cara's breath stilled. The concern and care in them was so deep and so warm that she felt unable to look away. He felt like a safe haven, a port in the middle of a storm. Why did he have such an effect on her? Before he could say anything else, his phone rang, breaking the connection.

Regret flooded his face as he retrieved his phone from his pocket. "Sorry, I have to get this."

As she watched him exit the living room, her heart fluttered in her chest. She needed to get a hold of herself. She had no time for relationships and certainly not with a man who had come here believing she was a suspect.

🦋 10 🦋

COLE

As soon as he ended the call, Cole grabbed his laptop from his room and returned to the living room where Cara was immersed in her own screen. "You have a minute?" he asked as he set his laptop on the coffee table.

She glanced up at him. "I can. What's up?"

"That was my lab tech, Wendy. She analyzed more of the items from the crime scene and sent them over. I thought that since you knew Steve better than I did that you might look at them with me to see if we can discover anything."

Cara narrowed her gaze at him. Was she too busy or did she perhaps think that he still considered her a suspect and was hoping she would reveal herself?

"Sure." She closed her own laptop and moved where she could see Cole's better.

He cued up the pictures of the crime scene that Wendy had sent. Cara winced as the first shot with the blood splatter pulled up. "Sorry." He clicked past it quickly. It must have been hard for her to find her associate.

"Wait, what was that?" Cara pointed at Cole's screen and moved her finger in a rewind motion.

Cole clicked to go back to the previous picture. The photo appeared on the screen and Cole leaned closer. "What is that?" The photo displayed a small gold circular item, but he wasn't exactly clear what it was.

Cara leaned closer as well. "Is that a cufflink?"

A cufflink? Cole had never worn them, so he wasn't too familiar with them, but he supposed it was possible. "Was Steve the type to wear cufflinks?"

Cara shook her head. "I don't know. He never wore them at work, but we had to split up about a year ago. Maybe he got into them during that time? Are there any pictures of the shirts in his closet?"

Cole clicked forward to see if Wendy had taken pictures of Steve's shirts. Sure enough, the next few pictures displayed a variety of long-sleeved shirts, but none of them had cufflinks.

"It doesn't appear it came from any of his shirts," Cara said, "at least not any in his closet."

Nodding, Cole clicked to return the cufflink to the

screen. "So, maybe the person who attacked him left it? Is there something on it?" He hit the zoom button to enlarge the photo and squinted. Though the image grew grainy, it appeared to be a snake on the gold circle.

"Is that a snake?" Cara asked as she leaned closer.

"I think so. Does that mean anything to you?"

"No, but it at least gives us something to look for."

11

CARA

Cara was knee deep in epitope research when her cell phone rang. She had honestly been expecting it a lot sooner - she'd given her number to everyone at the meeting a few days earlier and told them to call her at the first sign of anything, but the last few days had been quiet. Quiet and nerve wracking.

She'd spent the mornings researching and sitting on pins and needles waiting for a call. Then Cole or Makenna would force her outside for some air and time off her computer. She would agree and spend some time outdoors soaking in the sun and trying not to check her phone until she couldn't stand not helping any longer. Then, she would go back inside and stare at the screen for another few hours.

She hadn't realized what a toll the waiting and not

knowing had taken on her until she felt the tension in every fiber of her body at the ringing of the phone. Snatching it from its place beside her computer, she punched the call button without looking at the caller ID. It didn't really matter who was calling. "This is Cara."

"Cara? It's Nick. I think we might have our first case over here at the hospital. I've already alerted Jack Stone, but I thought you and Cole might like to come interview the victim too."

And there it was. The other shoe. Though she had been waiting for it to drop, this was her worst fear come true. She hadn't wanted to be right about the virus being released on Fire Beach, but she hadn't wanted it to get released elsewhere either. Perhaps it would be a false alarm. Maybe the case would just be pneumonia or the flu. "Yes, we'll be right there."

Cole looked up from his spot across the room. He had been poring over the crime scene photos again as if something new would magically appear. "Has it begun?"

A swift nod was all she could manage. "Nick thinks so, but if this is the first case, it won't take long depending on how it was started. If they got it in the food or water supply..." She trailed off, unable to finish the thought.

Cole was by her side in an instant. His hand touched her arm, sending a jolt of electricity through her. "Hey, let's not think like that. Nick said they had the medicine on hand, right?"

"Yes, but if it mutated…" Again words failed her.

"You said that takes time, right?"

His hand moved up and down her arm, causing her concentration to falter even more. She nodded.

"Good. Then let's not jump to the worst-case scenario just yet, okay? We assess and then we act, right?"

Assess and then act. She let the words wash over her and offered him a ghost of a smile. Cole had been refreshing to have around the last few days. Not only was he smart, but he had this calming influence, and while Cara didn't often get spun up, knowing she had put her friends at risk had shortened her fuse.

Squaring her shoulders, she took a deep breath and lifted her chin. "You're right. We check it out and then we panic if necessary." She offered the last part with a little humor and was rewarded with the wide smile that crossed Cole's features.

"Panic is never necessary."

He squeezed her arm before letting go to grab his coat, and she immediately missed the warmth of his touch. What was she doing? This was no time to be falling for anyone, even someone as handsome and intelligent as Cole.

"You ready?" He paused at the door and turned to her.

No, she wasn't ready, but would she ever be? She issued a curt nod and followed him out of the room.

The ride to the hospital was short and tense. Neither of them spoke, and Cara wished she had words to say, but for the first time in her life, they failed her. A sense of guilt that this was all her fault was the only thing she could think about.

She pulled into a spot and turned off the ignition, but before she could remove the key, Cole placed a hand on hers. Her gaze locked with his.

"It's going to be okay."

His words were so confident, but she couldn't find comfort in them. This wasn't his mess. These weren't his friends.

"What if it's someone I know?" The voice that came out of her mouth was so soft and scared that she barely recognized it as her own.

"The doctors here are good, right?"

Cara nodded. Though she didn't know them well, they appeared to be knowledgeable and efficient.

"Then we trust that they will do everything they can to help whoever it is. Whatever they can't do, God will cover."

She blinked at him. Hearing him mention God was certainly unexpected as was the way he said it - as if God was a friend and not some supernatural being no one had ever seen. Curiosity burned within her, but now was not the time. Hopefully there would be time for questions later.

"Thank you."

He smiled slightly and after a moment, removed his hand so they could exit the car.

At the front desk, they asked the nurse to page Nick, and a moment later he appeared - face grim and concerned. "Come with me."

Those three short words filled Cara with dread as she followed Nick toward the ICU.

"Even though you said it wasn't transmitted person to person, we went ahead and put him in isolation just in case." Nick flashed his badge to open a sealed door. "Here's what's odd though. After you spoke with us, I did some research and this disease has a crazy timeline. Symptoms can show up within a day or take years - there doesn't even appear to be rhyme or reason to the timeline - but the average is at least a week after exposure."

Cara's brow furrowed as she counted back the days. "But my break-in was only a few days ago."

"Exactly, which brings me to my point. I don't think our friend was infected here. Especially with how advanced his case seems. You'll need to suit up before we can go inside."

Cara and Cole followed his instructions, donning the hazmat gear before following him into the room. The gear was bulky and awkward, and though she knew it was for her protection, Cara felt like a character in a science fiction movie as she stepped through the doorway.

A single bed occupied the room - a man, pale and quiet, lay beneath the sheet. The electronic hum of a monitor and the periodic beeping of some machine broke the eerie silence of the room.

"He presented with a cough, a high fever, and incoherent ramblings. Thanks to your briefing we decided to run a urine and blood test. He has since become delirious fading in and out of consciousness. We're still waiting for the blood test to come back, but I have no doubt it will show the illness is in his bloodstream."

As Cara stared at the man, an itch tickled her brain. He appeared familiar, but she couldn't quite place his face. Of course that probably had to do with his color and lack of animation, but she couldn't help but think that if she could place him, it might answer a whole lot of questions.

Suddenly, the man's eyes shot open. They jumped from person to person, finally landing on Cara, and his face shifted as if he recognized her. "I'm sorry."

Cara stepped forward. "For what?"

"Everything." He opened his mouth to say more, but his eyes closed before any other sound came out.

"I think he needs rest." Nick touched her arm. "Maybe we can try again later when the medicine kicks in?"

Cara nodded, but she hoped there would be a later. She knew how deadly this disease could be, and if he were already feverish, it meant it had to be in his bloodstream.

12

COLE

Cole watched as Cara's eyes lingered on the unconscious man even as they stepped out of the room and a nurse helped them remove their gear. She knew something; he could tell from the slight tensing of her jaw and the folding under of her bottom lip.

"What do you have him on?" she asked the doctor.

"Ceftazidime," the doctor replied, "but it's too early to tell if it's working. I just started him on it half an hour ago."

"Did he check himself in or was he brought in?"

"Brought in. We don't even have his name. Still searching for some identification. The woman who brought him in is out in the waiting room if you want to talk to her. I don't think she knows him, but she seemed determined to stay until she knew he was okay."

The vein in Cara's neck pulsed as she nodded. "Thanks, Nick. Keep me informed if you can. If he does test positive, we need to call the CDC."

He nodded. "Already have the number programmed in my cell phone."

The vein popped a little more as Cara's lips mashed together. "Thanks, Nick."

When they were free of their gear, the nurse led them to the sanitizing area, so they could wash their hands. Questions burned in Cole's throat, but he waited until they were cleared and out of earshot to pose them.

"What aren't you saying?"

Cara inhaled deeply and scratched at her forehead. "I don't know exactly. The timeline bothers me for one. Nick is right that this disease seems to have no set timeline, but to already be in his bloodstream? That makes me think he could have had it when he attacked me and killed Steve which also seems unlikely."

"Would he not have had the strength?" Cole wasn't as familiar with this disease as Cara was, but if it was as serious as she claimed, he could see why she would be confused.

Her hand traveled to the back of her neck and rubbed absently. "I mean I suppose it's possible he would have the strength, but I don't see how he could have sneaked up on me if he had a cough. Also, if he had it before he attacked Steve, then where did he get it? Steve had the samples of the live virus and the infected mice. Something just doesn't feel right."

"Is it possible he infected himself stealing the virus from Steve and just progressed rapidly?"

"It's possible, especially if he has some underlying condition. I've read of people that showed symptoms within a day and others that didn't show symptoms for over fifty years. That's another thing that makes this disease so dangerous." She shook her head as if trying to grab a fleeting thought. "I suppose I need to do more research when we get back to the B&B."

Cole knew she would do just that. The woman was meticulous from everything he'd seen the last few days. Even her work station was never cluttered. Everything had a place and the desk was wiped down after every use. "That's not all though, is it?"

A frustrated breath passed over her lips. "No. That man in there seems familiar and he looked at me as if he recognized me, but I can't place whether I know him from here or somewhere else. Of course it doesn't help that he looks so pale right now."

Cole placed a hand on her arm. Along with her meticulousness, Cara had a trait of beating herself up over things she didn't get quickly or couldn't control. It was something he understood, but he also understood how that trait could eat away at you. "It will come to you. Why don't we go talk to the woman? Maybe she can help us figure out who he is."

Cara flashed a brief smile and squeezed his hand before returning the way they'd come. Cole paused at the nursing station, intending to ask who had brought the man in, but Cara continued to the waiting room. When he caught up to her, he realized why. Only one woman was in the room. Her head was tilted down, sending her dark locks fanning across her face and hiding her features.

"Excuse me, Miss?"

Cara's voice was softer than he had ever heard it. So, she did possess a compassionate side. He'd only seen the stronger sides of her - the stubborn, take charge, no nonsense sides. Though he had found her attractive before, he found his attraction to her increasing with every new piece he discovered.

The woman lifted her head. Wide brown eyes stared up at them. "Yes?" Her voice was softer than Cara's and held a note of... defeat?

"Are you the woman who brought in the man with the fever?"

The woman nodded. "I don't know him, but he was all alone, and I don't think anyone should be all alone. I told them I wanted to stay until I found out how he was doing. Do you know?"

Cole not only heard the desperation in her words, but he could see it in the woman's face. Though young, there were wrinkles by her eyes and along the corners of her mouth that hinted at the rougher hand she'd been dealt. He had no doubt from the way her hands continually twisted that she was speaking from experience, and the investigator in him wondered what her story was.

"I know Dr. Pearson has him on some medicine that should help him. My name is Cara Hunter, and this is my friend Cole Davenport. Do you think we could ask you some questions about earlier?"

The woman's thin shoulders lifted and then fell. "I guess so."

Cara smiled as she sat down in the seat next to the woman. "Can you tell us where you found the man?"

"He was outside the church, walking through the garden. I thought that was odd because usually the only people I see out there are the pastor or the women who run the food pantry. I approached him to ask who he was, but he was rambling some sort of nonsense about a woman named Sarah. I asked him who she was, but before he answered me, he fell to the ground. He was too heavy to lift and no one was around, so I called an ambulance."

"That was the right thing to do," Cara said, touching the woman's arm. "You probably saved his life. You said he was in the garden though. Was he doing anything? Carrying anything?"

"Um." The woman squeezed her eyes shut as if trying to conjure a mental memory. "Yes, he had a watering can, but I don't remember the ground being wet." Her eyes opened and she looked at Cara and then Cole. "Maybe he hadn't started watering yet?"

The cold sliver of dread coursed through Cole, and as he caught Cara's eyes, he knew she was thinking the same thing. Had he been poisoning the garden? Or had he become delirious before he'd started?

"Thank you. I just have one more question for now. Can you tell me which church?"

"Yeah, the Baptist one on Main."

When the vein pulsed in Cara's neck again, Cole knew that was not the information she had been hoping to hear.

"Thank you." Cole pulled a card from his wallet as he spoke up for the first time. "If you remember anything else, will you call us?"

The woman looked at him, nodded, and tucked the card in her pocket before dropping her head again.

"We have to go now," Cara hissed as they moved away from the woman. "That church? It's the biggest one in town, and that garden not only supplies the food pantry, but there's a group of volunteers who tend it. If that food goes out or even if they touch the soil, we'll have a lot more cases on our hands."

The dread grew within Cole as they reached the car. He could only hope they would get there in time.

☙ 13 ❧

CARA

Cara gripped the steering wheel to keep her hands from shaking. If he had managed to poison the garden, how many people would get infected? And what if that hadn't been his first stop? Could he have poisoned other places around town?

All of those questions bothered her, but the thing that bothered her the most was his face. He was familiar, and she didn't think it was from her bed and breakfast, but she couldn't place him. Perhaps if she could, that would help her figure out who was behind this.

"How big is this church?" Cole asked beside her as she turned down the last street.

"It's not one I attend, but I think it holds about three hundred, and it's the biggest donator to the food pantry." As she finished her sentence, the crosses that stood atop the large church came into view. Beside her, Cole let out a low whistle.

"You weren't kidding."

The church only stretched about three stories tall, but the expanse of it was mainly in the width. It spanned nearly an entire block, and the fear gripped Cara a little tighter as she pulled into the parking lot and saw the other cars. It wasn't a Sunday or a Wednesday, so she doubted they were here for service. She supposed they could belong to the employees, but she had no idea how many people worked in the church.

As soon as the car was in park, she killed the engine and shot out of the car. Cole quickly fell into step beside her.

Though large double doors under a covered entrance were directly in front of them, Cara veered to the right where she suspected the garden might lay. Sure enough, the planted rows soon came into view.

As she scanned the area, she called out for Cole to keep his eyes open for the watering can, but not to touch it if he found it. Before they had made it very far into the rows, a voice spoke up behind them.

"Can I help you?"

Cara turned to see a woman approaching them. Her short gray hair stood in contrast to her bright blue jump-suit. Though she appeared older than Cara, her thin build suggested she kept in shape, and she was definitely fashion conscious.

"Yes, ma'am. I'm Cara Hunter. I own the bed and breakfast near the beach-"

The woman's eyes lit up. "Oh, I've heard such great things about that place. It's so nice to meet you." She extended her hand, complete with a colorful shell bracelet, but Cara didn't shake it.

"I'm sorry. I don't mean to be rude, but we need to know if anyone has been in the garden recently."

The woman dropped her hand, a hesitant smile on her face as if she was unsure what to make of Cara's rudeness. "Well, yes. We just finished pulling the vegetables, and we're washing them in the kitchen. Did you need something?"

Cara's heart tightened. "Did anyone find a watering can?"

"I think Daisy did. She brought it in the church. Did you leave it?"

Cara exchanged a look with Cole, who had come to stand beside her. "No, but we might know who did. We need to speak with everyone who has been in the garden today or touched any of the food that came out of it."

The woman's hesitant demeanor dissolved into one of trepidation. "Are we in trouble?"

"Not trouble ma'am," Cole said, stepping forward with his hands up, "but possibly danger."

Her hand flew to her mouth as a shocked gasp passed her lips. "Come with me. I'll introduce you to everyone. I'm Martha, by the way."

"Martha, it's a pleasure to meet you. I wish we were here under better circumstances."

Cara marveled at how pleasant and calm Cole sounded. She prided herself on her cool head in the face of danger, but she knew her voice and her manner generally reflected that coolness. She'd been called an ice queen more than once during her time in the military. Perhaps, she could pick Cole's brain after this was all over and find out how he was able to come across calm and kind.

The church kitchen was larger than her own kitchen back home and the sight of the ten women washing the vegetables and laughing together filled her with sadness. She hoped none of them would get ill, especially since it appeared the median age among them was over sixty. Cara knew the immune system often grew weaker with age.

"Martha? Is everything okay?" One woman stepped away from the counter as the trio entered. She reminded Cara of the grandmotherly stereotype. There was a slight blue tint to her curly hair and her shirt and slacks could have come directly from Betty White's Golden Girls wardrobe.

"I'm not sure." Martha turned to Cole and Cara as if indicating they should take over the conversation.

"Hi ladies." Cole flashed a charming smile at the

women. "My name is Cole Davenport, and this is Cara. We're here with some unfortunate news. It appears that someone got a hold of a virus. That person is in the hospital, but we have reason to believe he may have infected the soil of the garden you were working in."

The women's eyes widened, and several of them gasped. "What does that mean?" Betty White asked.

"I'm going to let Cara discuss that as she's more familiar with this virus." He looked to Cara and motioned with his head for her to step up.

Cara cleared her throat as she looked out at the fearful women. "This virus is Melioidosis. It's not a virus we often see in the states, and it's not generally transmitted person to person."

"Thank Heavens," another woman said as she fanned her face.

Cara bit the inside of her lip, hesitant to rain on the woman's parade. "Unfortunately, this virus is transmitted through soil and water."

The woman's smile slid from her face. "So, what are you saying?"

"I'm saying you all need to come with us to the hospital to get tested. If you touched the soil, you may be at risk of contamination."

Another woman lifted a weathered hand in the air. She appeared to be the oldest from her white hair and soft skin.

"What if you didn't touch the soil directly, but you touched something that was in the soil?"

"Like the vegetables?" Cara asked.

She nodded. "Yes, but before they were washed."

"What are you talking about Edith? No one has touched the vegetables except us."

Edith fidgeted nervously. "Well, actually, little Robbie came by, and I gave him some broccoli and potatoes for his family."

There was a collective sigh joined with a chorus of "Oh, Edith" from the women. Evidently this was something the woman did often.

"I'm sorry, but who is little Robbie?" Cara asked. Her cool demeanor had returned and she forced a smile to her face in an attempt to lighten it.

"He's a little boy who lives in the neighborhood," Martha said. "He has a very big family and they use the pantry a lot. Usually his mother comes by, but sometimes she sends Robbie and Edith sends him home with extra food or, in this case, early food."

"But you gave it to him before you washed it?" Cara asked.

Edith nodded. "Is he in danger too?"

"I'm afraid he could be. Does anyone know where he lives?"

The women looked at each other and shook their heads

before Edith spoke up again. "I know what direction he went, but we've never actually been to his house."

Cara resisted the urge to rake her hand through her hair. She had been hoping they would be able to contain the outbreak here, but it appeared they were too late. "How about a last name?" If she had that, at least she could get Jordan involved. Maybe he could look the family up. She knew he was more familiar with the area than she was.

Edith pursed her lips, sending more wrinkles out from her mouth and across her forehead. "Um, I think it's Robertson. I remember it was like Robertson because that's my son-in-law's last name, but it wasn't exact."

"No, I'm pretty sure it's Peterson," another woman spoke up. This one had flaming red hair that screamed it came from a bottle and not the good Lord.

"I thought it was Richardson," Martha spoke up. "Isn't the mother's name Dotty?"

"No, Darla."

Cara wondered how these women got anything done. It appeared none of them had a great memory, and they were now bickering like hens in a yard. She held up her hands. "Ladies, it's fine. Those names are helpful. I have a friend in the police department, and he can look them up. I'm sure he'll find Robbie. Now if you can please come to the hospital with Cole and me. It really is important that we get you tested."

Her words were like a bucket of water on a flame. The

women immediately hushed, and the tone grew somber. Cara bit back a sigh. This was not her strong suit at all.

"Ladies, get your keys. We have work to do," Martha said, coming to her rescue.

As the other women buzzed around, grabbing their purses and other things, Cara stepped closer to Martha. "Thank you."

Martha nodded. "I know you're just trying to do your job. They're all a little rattled right now, but they're good women."

Cara placed a hand on the woman's shoulder. "I know they are. Do you know where the watering can is?"

A blank look covered Martha's face for a moment before she perked up and motioned Cara to follow her to the back of the kitchen. There, on a small table near the back door, sat the offensive item. Cara looked around for something to pick it up with. She wasn't afraid of contamination from the can, but she didn't want to smear any fingerprints or add her own.

"Here."

She turned to find Cole holding out a medical glove to her. The corners of her lips pulled up slightly. "You always carry one of those around with you?" This man was full of surprises.

He shrugged. "I was a Royal Ranger growing up. Always gotta be prepared."

Cara had never heard of the Royal Rangers, but she

assumed they were akin to Boy Scouts or the like. She took the glove and offered a small smile. "Thank you. Guess I could learn a few lessons from you."

"I'd be happy to teach you anything I can."

He'd appeared to say the words without thinking, but something crackled in the air between them as their gazes locked. A warmth that Cara hadn't felt in a long time sprouted in her heart.

"If you two are ready," Martha said, interrupting the moment, "we are too."

"Yes, of course." Cara shook her head to clear it, grabbed the can, and led the way to the parking lot. What had she been thinking? She was in the middle of what could turn into an outbreak. She had no time to be developing feelings for the man who had initially come to arrest her. So why couldn't she get him out of her mind?

14

COLE

"Do you think you could find your way back to the hospital?" Cara asked as they approached her car.

Cole blinked at her. "Are you leaving me here?"

"What? No," Cara shook her head, a small smile pulling at the corners of her lips, "I need to call Jordan, so I was offering to let you drive. Talking while driving is frowned upon." She wiggled her cell phone as if to emphasize her point.

Despite the heavy situation around them, Cole couldn't help but smile back at the feisty woman. She was quickly earning a place in his heart with her confident words and straightforward attitude. That was certainly refreshing after the last relationship he had been in. Not that this was a relationship…

"Yes, I can find my way back to the hospital." He needed to keep his rambling thoughts in check or he might find himself distracted from his real duty. Finding Sergeant Steele's killer.

"Great." She clicked the button to unlock the car and then tossed him the keys. Before he could say another word, she had her phone pressed to her ear. "Jordan? It's Cara. I need a favor."

Cole tried not to be jealous as he listened to Cara's conversation with Jordan. He didn't know if they were together, and he certainly had no claim on her, but he found himself hoping they were just friends.

"So, how long have you known Jordan?" Hoping his tone sounded nonchalant, he tossed the question at Cara as she placed her cell back in her pocket. He could feel her gaze turn to him, but he kept his eyes focused on the road.

"A few years. I met him once briefly when I was active in the military. He always spoke so highly of Fire Beach that when I had to come up with a cover, I suggested some-thing here."

"And do you still like it here?" Cole hoped her answer would give him some sort of clue as to her relationship status.

"I do. The people are amazing, and the beach is pretty nice too."

"Do you go there often?" How could he phrase his words so that he could get his answer without her knowing what he was attempting? From the corner of his eye, he saw her shake her head.

"Not as often as I'd like to. Work at the bed and breakfast keeps me busy, and it seems lately as if someone is always asking me to help them out. A few months ago, Jordan asked me to protect this woman Tia who had lost her memory, and just recently Tia asked me to shelter a woman who was running from an abusive boyfriend. Actually, she was our hostess at the restaurant the other day. I shouldn't complain though. They've all become great friends."

Friends. That was certainly something Cole didn't have enough of. At least not enough close ones. His lonely life was just one of many reasons he was considering a career change.

"I just hope I haven't put them all in danger," Cara continued.

He chanced a single glance at her. "We'll do everything we can. Did Jordan know the boy?"

"No, but he was going to ask around the department. Hopefully somebody will recognize the names." She sighed as she turned her face away from him and out the passenger window.

When they reached the hospital, Cole and Cara waited until all the women were out of their cars as well before leading them into the large building.

Nick met them at the receptionist desk. It appeared Jordan had called ahead warning him of incoming patients.

"All of these women were exposed?" Nick's eyes roamed from one woman to the next.

"We're not sure. They were all working in the garden where the other patient was spotted. I also brought his watering can. Is there a lab where I can run tests on it? That will help us determine if they were exposed as well."

Nick blinked at her, his words coming out in a stammer. "Uh, yeah." Turning to the nurse at the desk, he began issuing orders to get the women taken care of. "I'll show you to the lab really quick, but then I have to get back. This creates a larger need for isolation than we've ever needed before."

"Of course." Cara nodded and she and Cole followed Nick down to the laboratory section of the hospital.

After a quick introduction with the technician on duty, Nick excused himself to return to the women. Cara quickly began gathering items from around the lab. Though Cole was enjoying watching her work, he felt completely out of his element at the moment.

"Can I do anything to help?"

"Yeah, grab me some swabs," Cara said without looking in his direction.

He scanned the area, unsure of where they might be, and was saved when the technician pointed him in the right direction. Grabbing the swabs, he returned to Cara's side and watched as she set up the equipment she would need.

When she was satisfied that she had everything organized, she grabbed the swabs from him and began wiping different parts of the can. Then the swabs were placed into another machine. Cole had no idea what any of them did, but he found the process fascinating.

After a few more procedures he didn't understand, Cara slipped slides under a microscope. At least this part he understood. He hadn't enjoyed much of science in high school, but studying items under a microscope had been the one exception to that. He'd always looked forward to those days. In fact, when he was done with the assignment, he'd often grabbed random items from the floor or the room just to see what they looked like magnified.

"Darn it." Cara's words were little more than a soft sigh before she pushed her chair back.

"Can I see?" Cole hesitated to ask, not wanting to sound too eager but curious to see for himself.

"Sure." She scooted a little farther away so that he could lean over the microscope.

He stepped closer, trying to ignore the heat he felt from the closeness of her body. In the microscope, he could see the spiky spheres that were signatures of most viruses. He blew out his breath in a frustrated huff. "Okay, so we know the can was contaminated."

"Yeah, we just don't know what else was. Come on, we

better go see if any of the women have tested positive." She stood up and glanced toward the lab technician. "Can you leave this here until we come back?"

"Sure." The lab technician was too involved in her own work to have paid them much attention, and Cole doubted she would get around to moving Cara's stuff.

They were almost to the entrance of the lab when suddenly Cara froze. Her whole body stiffened, and her mouth dropped open as her eyes widened. For a second, Cole feared she was having some sort of reaction. "What's wrong? Are you okay?"

She turned her fear-filled eyes on him. "I know who patient zero is."

❧ 15 ❧

CARA

Cara couldn't believe she hadn't remembered the man immediately when she'd seen him. Of course, he'd looked different than the last time she had seen him, wild eyed and ranting as security dragged him away, but there had been so few interruptions at their lab while they had been in the lab that he should have come to mind immediately.

"So, who is he?" Cole asked.

"His name is David Grissom. He was an intern at the lab shortly before we went undercover." Cara paused as the past flooded into her mind.

"What are you working on Lieutenant Hunter?"

Cara smiled at the young intern. He'd been placed with them only a week ago, but he seemed eager to learn. The shaggy cut of his sandy brown hair added to his youthful appearance as did his doe like brown eyes though they were often hidden behind his glasses. "I'm trying to isolate parts of the virus so I can study possible vaccine options."

"That sounds fascinating. Have you found anything yet?"

He pushed his glasses up on his nose, and Cara couldn't help noticing that he seemed nervous. But perhaps what she thought was nerves was really excitement.

"Not yet," Steve piped up from the other side of the room. "This virus is proving to be tricky."

David swallowed, and it seemed almost audible to Cara as she watched a droplet of sweat trickle down the side of his face. It wasn't that warm in the room, so why was he sweating?

"But you're going to, right? Soon?" His voice had risen higher than his normal pitch, and Cara took a step toward him.

"David? Are you okay?"

He turned wild eyes on her and then took a deep breath as if realizing how crazy he sounded. "I'm fine. Of course. Just hoping we find a vaccine soon."

Cara glanced over at Steve and saw him moving his hand slowly under his desk. Malone had installed panic buttons under their desks that allowed them to alert security if anyone got into the lab who wasn't supposed to. Cara had never thought they would actually need to use the alarm, much less against one of their own. She gave him an imperceptible nod, her silent assent, before turning back to David. Perhaps if she could diffuse this, they could all laugh about it later.

"David, what's going on? We told you this was a long process when you first joined us."

He ran his hand through his hair and took another shaky breath. After a moment, he appeared to calm slightly. "I know, but I thought it would be faster. People's lives are at stake, you know?"

"We do know, and we are working as hard as we can." She looked up as Security entered the lab. "David, these men are going to escort you out of here for now. I think you need a break."

His eyes turned wild again as the security officers stepped toward him. "What? No! I have to stay! I have to know what's going on!"

Cara and Steve watched with wide eyes as David continued to yell and fight the guards as they dragged him out of the room.

"Well, that was weird," Steve said when the silence descended again.

"To say the least. What was that all about?" Cara couldn't shake the feeling that there was more going on than what it seemed.

"Who knows? Maybe the pressure of college got to

him." He bent back over the microscope as if that was the answer and therefore the conversation was over.

Maybe, but Cara wasn't so sure. She'd have to make sure Malone knew about this.

"And did you tell Malone?" Cole asked when she finished recounting the story.

"Yeah. He seemed surprised by David's actions, but that was the last time we saw David, and the last time we had an intern. I always assumed Malone fired him. In fact, it was shortly after that incident that Malone informed us we had a leak and needed to separate. I need to call him and let him know. Plus, I'd like to make sure CDC knows about our situation."

Cole nodded. "I'll give you some space while I check on the women."

"Thank you. I appreciate it." Cara watched Cole disappear down the hallway before pulling out her cell phone. Questions raced through her head as she dialed Malone's number. Who was David really? And had he stolen their research? Had he been the one to kill Steve?

"Cara." Malone's deep voice flooded the phone after the second ring. He didn't even bother with the normal pleasantries. "Have you found anything out?"

"A little. There's a man who's taken ill here, and I'm fairly certain it's David Grissom."

"Who?" The word came out a little squeakier than Cara would have expected.

"David Grissom. You know the intern we had for about a week? I assumed you fired him after he got all weird that one day."

"Oh, right." Something in his voice didn't sit right with Cara, but she wasn't exactly sure what it was. "You say he's there?"

"He is, and as he appears to be the first person sick, I'm fairly certain he was trying to poison the town though his case seems advanced. He was seen in a food garden with a watering can. The can was positive for Melioidosis."

"The first? How many are there?"

Cara narrowed her eyes as her instincts prickled even further. Why did he sound more excited than concerned? "None so far, but there were several elderly ladies who were in the garden after David. They've just come in for testing. I was about to call the CDC and inform them of our cases unless that's something you need to do?"

"The CDC? Yeah, I can call them, but they generally don't come out until there's officially an outbreak, and with your one case, I don't think it qualifies yet. However there is guidance you can follow posted on their website."

Anger flooded Cara. "What? Do they know how fast this virus can spread if it gets in the food or water supply? And how deadly it is? By the time we have an outbreak, it may be too late to do anything about it."

"It's procedure, Cara, but I'll call them now that you have a confirmed patient, and we'll see what they say."

"Please. I need some help here, Malone. Without Steve, I'm now trying to find a vaccine all on my own along with trying to save the people of this town. Were you able to secure me any more help yet?"

"Not yet. You just focus on the vaccine. I'll take care of the rest."

Cara rolled her eyes. How exactly was he going to take care of the rest from his office across the country? "Okay, Malone, I have to go. I'm going to check on the women, but I'll call back in later."

As she hung up the phone, she couldn't help but wonder if Malone was distracted by something where he was. He certainly hadn't seemed overly concerned with her plight here, and now she felt more alone than before. At least Cole seemed to believe her and had stopped looking at her like she might be a suspect. In fact, a few times she had even caught him looking at her like he considered her a friend. Or more.

Whoa! She had to get her thoughts under control. Cole might be easy on the eyes, but she could not be thinking about that right now. Not with a virus spreading through her town.

COLE

ole stared at the frail looking man in the hospital bed and tried to process what he had just learned. If the intel he had received was true, the man's actions were understandable. Not justifiable, but understandable.

"Any news on the women?"

Cole turned to see Cara striding his direction. Her face wore an even more worried expression than when he'd left her, and he wondered how the call with her boss had gone. "The women have all been admitted while they wait on the blood test results, but no news so far. At least not on them."

Cara's brow furrowed. "What do you mean?"

Cole turned back toward the glass that looked into the

hospital room. "I did manage to find out some information on your friend in there."

A derisive scoff escaped Cara's thin lips. "He's no friend of mine. Especially not if he's the one who killed Steve, attacked me, and stole our research."

"I can understand that, but I called in a few favors. It turns out David here has been receiving quite a few large payments over the last year."

"For what?" Curiosity threaded Cara's voice though her face remained impassive.

"That's a good question, but my guess would be that he was helping someone. Someone or some group with large pockets who wanted intel on your project. There's more though."

"More? What more could there be?" Anger flashed in Cara's eyes, and Cole knew he better tread lightly.

"It turns out that David's sister has a rare form of cancer. She was diagnosed shortly before he became an intern for you if my timeline is correct, so my guess is that his actions are about getting the money to pay for his sister's cancer treatments."

Cara crossed her arms and fixed him with an icy stare. If looks could kill, he would have been incinerated on the spot from her gaze. "I don't care what the reason for his actions are. He killed Steve, and his actions may kill many in this town."

"It's certainly not justifiable, I agree."

"It's madness is what it is. I just hope he lives, so I can interrogate him and go after the people or person who sent him on this mission."

"I get your frustration, but we don't know for sure that he killed Steve. Did he seem like the type to wear cufflinks?"

Cara opened her mouth to reply and then closed it. She blew out a harsh breath before raking her hand through her short hair. "No, he didn't, but I didn't know him very well. However, I also don't know many college kids who even know what cufflinks are." Another sigh escaped her lips. 'You know what? I need a break. I'm going to get a coffee and cool off a bit."

Cole watched her walk away and bit the inside of his lip. He wished he had the right words to say, but it seemed Steve had been like a partner to her. That kind of loss wasn't easy to recover from. He knew that all too well.

"Was that Cara I saw leaving?" Nick asked as he stepped out of David's room.

Cole nodded. "It was. I shared some information I learned about your patient, but her emotions are too raw right now. How's he doing by the way?"

Nick ran a hand across his jaw. "It's still early, but I think we may have gotten him the medicine in time. He certainly doesn't appear to be getting worse."

"That is good news. I know Cara would like to have a

few words with him when he wakes up." He folded his arms across his chest. "How about the women?"

"I'm on my way there now to check. Want to come with me?"

Cole had no reason to stand in the hallway alone, so he agreed and followed Nick toward the nurses' station. Before they reached it though, a loud worried voice carried their direction.

"We have a ten-year-old with a high fever and complaints of pain. Page Dr. Pearson."

Cole's heart sank. Though he hoped he was wrong, somehow, he just knew the youth in question was the one who had received the food from the kind, elderly woman.

"I'm here. Let's get him to room one. Stat."

As Nick disappeared with the nurses trailing after him, Cole noticed a thin blonde woman watching the scene. Her hand clutched tightly at her necklace, and the fear that radiated from her eyes seemed to create an almost perceptible cloud in front of her.

"Excuse me, are you the mother?"

The woman blinked at him a few times before nodding. "What's going on? Is he going to be okay? He came in about an hour ago complaining of stomach pain. I thought he was just trying to get out of his chores, but then the fever started."

Cole pursed his lips as he thought back to Cara's briefing and his own research on the disease. Could it spread that fast? If her son had touched or ingested the contaminated food, it would have only been in the last few hours. That seemed a rather fast timeline, but the alternative was an even scarier thought.

"Do you know if your son ate the food he brought home from the church today?"

Fear filled the woman's eyes, and she took a step away from him. "How did you know about that? Who are you?"

Cole sighed. Generally he was better at choosing his words, but his gut was telling him something was off. "My name is Cole Davenport. I'm a Criminal Investigator, and I think your son has been exposed to Melioidosis. We just came from the church where it appears someone poisoned the food, and Edith told us she gave some to Robbie. It's important we know where it came from. Can you tell me where he's been over the last week?"

"Melio what? What is that? Is it deadly?" Hysteria was creeping into the woman's voice and clouding her wide, frightened eyes. Cole knew he was running out of time to get answers.

"Dr. Pearson has the antibiotics on hand to help your son, but if I don't figure out where he was exposed, a lot more people might get sick. Can you help me out? Please?"

The woman blinked at him a few more times before running a shaky hand through her hair. "Um, well he went to the church this morning. Yesterday, he delivered newspapers in the morning and then he played with some friends. I'm sorry. I have a baby and several other children who need my attention during the day. Robbie is on his own a lot in the afternoons."

Cole's heart went out to the woman. He could see the stress of her situation weighing heavily on her heart, and he didn't want to make it any worse for her. Placing a hand on her arm, he offered a smile. "That's okay. Can you name one of his friends? I can go talk to them."

Relief at his lack of condemnation on her parenting skills covered her face, and she offered a slight smile in return. "Cecil Jacobs. That's Robbie's best friend. They do everything together."

"Thank you." Cole had no idea who Cecil Jacobs was, but he knew someone who would be able to find out. Now he just needed to find Cara.

17
CARA

Cara looked up as Cole strode her direction. A fierce intensity rolled off him like an invisible wave, and the hair on the back of her neck stood up. Something was wrong. "What's happened?" she asked when he was within ear shot.

"Little Robbie was just admitted."

Cara's brow furrowed. "So soon? That makes no sense. The incubation time is usually-"

"At least two days," he finished for her. "Which means he must have gotten it earlier this week."

Cara felt her stomach drop. If she had been standing, her knees would have given out beneath her. "So David managed to disperse it somewhere else, but we have no idea where? We have to alert the media."

Cole held up a hand. "Slow down. We may not know

where yet, but his mother was able to give me the name of his best friend. Evidently they do nearly everything together. If he's not sick yet, maybe we can figure out where Robbie was exposed."

Cara tilted back the last of her coffee and pushed her chair back. "What are we waiting for then? What's his friend's name?"

"Cecil Jacobs."

Cara was unfamiliar with the name, but she knew exactly how to find his address. After tossing her cup in the trash, she pulled out her cell phone, finger punching Jordan's speed dial number. "Jordan? It's Cara. I need an address."

Twenty minutes later they pulled up to a small rambler that appeared in dire need of some TLC. The paint peeled in large curls from the siding, and there was an obvious sag in the porch. As they opened their doors, Jordan pulled up behind them.

"You two will let me ask the questions, understand?"

Cara nodded. Though she hadn't expected Jordan to show up just to ask a kid a few questions, she did feel better having him there.

She and Cole fell into step behind Jordan and waited as he knocked on the door. A boy who looked to be about ten with sandy blond hair opened the door slightly and stared out at them.

"Hello, my name is Detective Graves. Are you Cecil

Jacobs?" Cara recognized Jordan's soothing voice - the one he always used when talking to kids or stressed out people. He had an imposing demeanor most of the time, but he could soften it and come across like a teddy bear when he wanted.

The boy's eyes narrowed as he took in Jordan's normal clothes instead of a uniform as well as Cara and Cole behind him. "Are you a real cop? Do you have a badge? And who are they?"

Cara pressed her lips together to keep from smiling. The kid was smart. She wasn't sure if he was home alone or not though she guessed he was, but his parents had obviously taught him well.

"I am a real cop. In fact, I'm going to reach in my pocket and pull out my badge."

This was another thing Jordan always did that Cara didn't hear many others do. He always explained what he was about to do so as not to take anyone by surprise. She'd seen many times in the military where surprised people acted instinctually and often got themselves or others hurt. She would bet he had seen his fair share as well.

After seeing his badge, the kid nodded his head slightly. "Okay, you're real, but who are they?"

"These are my friends. Cara here owns a bed and breakfast in town and Cole is a criminal investigator here on a case."

Jordan obviously thought honesty was the best policy

here, though Cara wasn't so sure how much the boy would understand. Evidently, whether he grasped it all or not, the explanation appeared to placate him. The door opened a little wider.

"I'm Cecil Jacobs. Did I do something wrong?"

Jordan shook his head. "Not at all. We're actually here because your friend Robbie is sick. We think he was exposed to a virus that's making him ill, and we're hoping you can tell us where you two have been the last few days."

Cecil's eyes widened. "Robbie is sick? Am I going to get sick too?"

This time Jordan turned to Cara. She took a small step forward but stayed behind Jordan. "We sure hope not, but it would be really helpful if you could tell us where you guys went this week."

The boy didn't seem entirely convinced, and he dodged her question with one of his own. "How would I know if I was sick?"

"It can be different for everyone, but the main symptoms would be a fever, cough, aches. It might feel like the flu. Have you had any of those symptoms?"

He shook his head. "Does that mean I'm okay?"

"It's very likely though I would love to get you tested just in case. Now, can you tell us where you went?"

The boy chewed on his bottom lip. "Well, yesterday we

went to the school and played around on the playground for most of the day, but the day before, we snuck into the community pool. It was really hot, and we just wanted to cool off."

The pool. Cara closed her eyes and tried not to show emotion. Why had she not thought of the pool? Though few people would drink the water, it could get in their system through their nose, ears, or any cuts. "Did you go in the water?"

"Robbie did. I can't swim, so I just stayed near the sprinkler lines." His eyes widened. "Do you think that's how he got sick?"

"It's very possible. Were there other people in the pool?"

Cecil nodded slowly. "Yeah, the place was packed."

Cara felt her heart drop. There was no telling when David had poisoned the water. How many people had been exposed?

"I'll call and get the pool shutdown. Maybe they have a way to track who's been there." Jordan was already pulling out his cell phone and walking away as he tossed the words at her.

Cara nodded and kept her eyes on Cecil who looked as if the gravity of the situation had finally hit him. "Cecil, are your parents here?"

He pursed his lips and shook his head. "They're both at work."

"Would you be okay if I call them and see if we can take you to the hospital for testing?"

He nodded, and when she held out her phone, he tapped the number in before handing it back to her. "That's my mom's number. Dad will never answer."

She wondered briefly what his father did that he couldn't answer a call from his kid who was home alone, but then her heart ached for parents who needed to both work and leave their young son home alone. She would have to ponder ways to help out families like his in the future.

After punching the call button, she held the phone to her ear and listened. There was only one ring before a woman in a hushed voice answered. "Hello?"

"Hello, is this Mrs. Jacobs?" She looked at Cecil with raised eyebrows, hoping to confirm that was in fact his mother's last name. She should have asked that first.

"Yes, who is this?"

"My name is Cara Hunter. You don't know me, but I'm here with Cecil-"

"Is he okay?" The woman's volume rose just a bit as fear flooded her voice. "Has he done something wrong?"

"No, he's done nothing wrong, and he's fine, but he may have been exposed to a virus. I'm calling to see if Detective Jordan Graves and I can take him to the hospital or if you can come home and take him in yourself." Cara didn't want to overstep. She didn't have kids, but she imagined she wouldn't be comfortable with some stranger claiming to take her son or daughter to a hospital. "It is important that he get tested."

As the silence dragged on, Cara knew the woman on the other end was weighing her options. "I'll see if I can take an extended break and bring him in."

It wasn't what Cara had hoped to hear, but she could understand the woman's hesitation. At least now that she knew where he lived, she could check on him or send someone from the hospital to do it if he didn't make it in. "That sounds like a plan. Thank you."

Cara ended the call and looked back at Cecil. "Your mom is going to try and come home to take you in to get tested. Please let her know it's important, okay?"

Cecil nodded.

"And no more sneaking into the pool. Especially not until we know it's safe."

He nodded again, a look of chagrin on his face.

"What now?" Cole asked after Cecil had gone back in the house and closed the door.

Cara sighed. She didn't know what the next step was. Holding a press conference? Getting the word to the media outlets? Checking on Robbie and the women? Continuing to work on the vaccine? "I'm not even sure."

18

COLE

Cole bit the inside of his lip as he studied Cara. The news of the day was certainly taking a toll on her. Dark circles now sat prominently beneath her eyes, and she had run her hand through her short hair so much that it stuck up in crazy directions.

"What if we take a break and get some food? You look like you could use a short rest."

She arched an eyebrow at him. "How can I think about taking a rest? I need David to wake up so I can question him; I need to find out who has been in the community pool; I need to find out if the CDC will show up and help us out; and I need to continue working to find a vaccine. How on earth can I even think about taking a break?"

Cole stepped forward and placed his hand on her arm. "It's because of everything you just said that you need to take a break. If you don't, you will exhaust yourself and you won't be able to do any of it. Then, where will we be?"

Cara opened her mouth to protest, but then acceptance flickered in her eyes. She knew he was right. "Fine. We can grab some lunch and then we need to get back to the hospital. I need to find out who David was working for. I don't suppose there was any name on those deposits you were able to find?"

Cole shook his head. "No, they came from an unknown source, but it's definitely someone with connections."

Jordan returned at that moment. "I got the pool closed and they do keep a log of most of the people who were there. Members have to scan a card to get in and visitors have to sign a log. However, if there were any more kids like Robbie and Cecil who snuck in-" He shrugged, letting his statement fade. They all knew what it would mean if there had been others.

"I'm going to get the log and then I'll start checking on people and sending them to the hospital."

"Can we help?" Cara asked.

"I think it would be better if police officers showed up with these questions. I'll call in the rest of the team to help. You should continue doing what you do best - research this stuff and find a cure. I'd love to say we lost no one."

Cara bit her lip and nodded. "Me too."

As Jordan walked off, Cole touched her arm again.

"Come on, let's get some food and then we can check on David again."

She let him lead her to the car, but he could tell her brain and energy were focused elsewhere. He couldn't blame her. Though none of this was her fault, it was her research that had brought the disease here which very well might claim the lives of people she knew. It was a heavy burden to bear.

"Fire Dreams again or is there some other place I should try?" Cole had enjoyed the food at Fire Dreams. He wouldn't mind going back, but he was always willing to try new places as well.

Cara shrugged. It appeared the fight had gone out of her with the frustrations over what to do next. Cole sighed but pointed the car in the direction of Fire Dreams. He didn't know the area well enough to drive around aimlessly, and he didn't trust the app on his phone to lead him to a good restaurant.

The same hostess who had seated them a few days ago greeted them with a smile as they entered. It faded slightly as she took in Cara's dark cloud, and she sent a questioning gaze in Cole's direction. He shook his head. Not even knowing this woman's name, he certainly didn't feel comfortable sharing the current troubles.

Thankfully, she took the hint and led them to a table near the back of the restaurant. After laying the menus down, she quietly excused herself, and Cole stared at Cara.

He didn't know her well, but he'd worked with enough people in his career to know that he needed to get her out of her funk as soon as possible.

"What made you join the military?" he asked as he opened the menu.

She glanced up at him. "Really? That's what you want to talk about right now with a pandemic on our hands?"

He folded his hands across the menu and fixed her with an intent gaze. "Yes, it's what I want to talk about right now because we need a moment that's not focused on the pandemic. Rest, remember?"

She held his gaze, and he could see her jaw muscles tensing as if she were about to argue with him. Instead, she rolled her eyes and sighed. "Fine. I joined the military because I was tired of getting picked on."

Cole furrowed his brow. Cara was the epitome of an athletic, muscular woman. He doubted she had much fat on her, and he'd seen her muscles as she moved. When had she been picked on?

"All through school, I was the chunky kid. My family wasn't overweight, so I was convinced I was adopted or had some medical condition that caused it. I was constantly picked on and had pretty poor self-esteem. When I went to college, it was originally to go into lab research. At least there, I thought I could blend in with the other nerds and finally fit in. Instead, I got saddled with a gung-ho ROTC roommate. She pestered me until I started running with her every morning and working out with her every evening. I started to see the weight come off even though my diet was still poor. Then she began teaching me nutrition and my whole life changed. I wanted to help people like she had helped me, and she told me about ROTC and how I could still do research but do it while serving my country."

Cara shrugged and opened her menu. "It seemed like the best of both worlds, so I signed up. Once I got in, I actually loved the structure and the rigor. I pushed myself even harder which is why David should never have gotten the jump on me at the house-"

Cole held up his hand to interrupt her. "Nope, no work talk right now. Rest, remember? How about your family? Are you still close with them?"

Cara narrowed her eyes at him. "Are you interrogating me now? I thought you'd decided I was innocent."

"I have." Cole bit back a sigh. Cara was definitely a tough case.

"Then what's with the third degree?"

"I just figured we haven't gotten to know each other well over the last few days because we've been so focused on work." He often found himself wishing at night before he lost his fight to sleep that he had gotten to know Cara better. She was intriguing but also a little like a cactus - sharp and prickly on the outside, but sweet inside. "Since we are taking a break from work. I thought we could take some time to learn about each other."

She stared at him but finally sighed. "No, I'm not really close with my family. We don't have much in common. The rest of my family never struggled with weight. In fact, my sister was homecoming and prom queen. I never really fit in."

Cole's heart ached for her, and he wondered if her past was part of the reason for her walls.

"In fact, that's probably why the people here have become like family which is why it's so important that none of them die."

At that moment, a squad car raced by the window, sirens and lights blaring. Cole and Cara both turned to watch it. He wondered if she was thinking the same thing he was. Before he could ask her though, another raced by the window and then another.

"What in the world?" Cole had only seen multiple cars at events a few times in his life and none of them had been good.

"They're heading toward the hospital. Come on, we have to go."

She bolted out of the booth before he could respond, and he sighed as his stomach growled. He had been hoping they would at least get a decent meal in before disaster struck again.

19

CARA

Cara knew it would be useless, but she tried dialing Jordan's number again. She needed to know what was going on, and her mental rebukes for taking a rest were playing over and over in her head. She should have gone back to the hospital. At least then she would have been there for whatever was happening.

Cole wasn't even able to reach the hospital parking lot before they were stopped by a cop. As he rolled down his window to speak to the woman, Cara realized all the entrances to the hospital were blocked. That could only mean a few things.

"I'm sorry, sir, this is an active crime scene and I'm going to have to ask you to turn around. If you need immediate medical attention, you'll need to go to Mercy Hospital on the east side of town."

Cole shook his head. "No, we have no medical emergency, but we are investigating a virus we know has at least one patient inside. Can you at least tell us if it involves that?"

"You can contact Detective Graves if you need to," Cara piped up from the passenger seat. "Tell him it's Cara Hunter and Cole Davenport."

The female cop offered a small smile. "No need ma'am. I recognize your name, but I can tell you it's not about the virus that I know of. We received a call for a Code Silver."

A Code Silver. Cara knew exactly what that meant. Someone with a weapon was inside the hospital, and while there was a possibility it could be for another reason, in her heart, she knew the person was after David. Whatever person or group he was working for would want him silenced before the police could interrogate him. The question was how did they even know he was here? There were only a few possibilities and none of them sat well with her.

"Thank you, Officer. When you see Jordan will you have him call me?" Cara asked.

The woman nodded. "Of course, ma'am."

Cole rolled up his window and turned away from the hospital, but he didn't drive very far before pulling over and turning to Cara. "Okay, what's a Code Silver?"

"It's the hospital's code for someone with a weapon." She said the words pointedly and waited for their meaning to sink in.

"And you think that someone is after David."

"It makes sense, right? Fire Beach isn't a small town and we have our fair share of crime, but the last time we had a code silver here was when evil people from out of town were after a woman who ended up here."

"So who would know David is here?"

Cara ran a hand through her hair and then realized she had done the gesture so often today that her short hair, while usually tidy, was bound to be a messy disaster. "That is the question that scares me. Either there were people here already watching to make sure he did what he was supposed to or they've got my phone bugged."

"Why would you say that?"

"I called my boss after we tested the watering can. Told him about David being admitted, but if they're bugging my phone, I have no idea what else they've heard." She shook her head as the frustration inside of her mounted.

"Cara, there is another possibility you should consider." Cole's voice was low and serious and it sent the hairs on her arm standing straight up.

"What's that?"

"Your boss could be in on this."

"What?" The very idea flabbergasted Cara. She'd

known Bradley Malone for years. He was the quintessential good guy. Played soccer with his kids, barbecued with his neighbors, never broke the law - not even for speeding. "Not Malone. He is patriotic to the core. He would never want to see innocent people killed by this virus." But even as she protested, the thought took hold in her mind. Could he have done that? He was the only one who knew where both she and Steve had moved to after the mole was discovered that she knew of. In fact, he'd been the one to tell them about the mole, but he couldn't be involved. The man bled red, white, and blue.

"Look, I'm not saying that he is, just that we shouldn't discount the possibility. Good people do bad things all the time for any number of reasons, right?"

She hated to acknowledge it, but he was right. David hadn't seemed like the type to commit murder either, but he'd apparently done so in order to help save his sister. Was it possible Malone had too?

Inside her pocket, her phone began buzzing. She pulled it out and hit the call button as soon as she recognized Jordan's number. "Jordan, what's going on in there?"

"I'm sorry, Cara. He's dead." Jordan's deep voice held a heavy sadness.

"David's dead? Did he say anything first? Did you at least get the guy who killed him?" Her voice took on a hysterical edge, and she realized she was almost yelling at him. She took a deep breath to try and calm herself. None of this was his fault.

"I'll ask Nick, but I don't think so. He was still sedated." Jordan paused and his breath was audible on the other end. "I'm afraid the shooter's dead too, Cara. Once he took out David, he turned the gun on us. It was self-defense."

"You let them kill him? How am I supposed to get answers now?"

Cole shot her a look, and Cara waved a dismissive hand at him. She knew she was being irrational; she just seemed unable to stop it. Her world had felt like a wobbly deck of card's house the last few days as it was. Now, one event had knocked it to the ground and sent the cards flapping around like injured birds.

There was a long pause on the other end, and Cara knew Jordan was composing himself. He'd never seen her this wound up - she couldn't remember the last time she had been this wound up - but he knew she was not herself. "I'm sorry, Cara. We'll look into the shooter, and we'll find out who's behind this one way or another. I promise."

Cara closed her eyes and took a deep breath. When she spoke again, her voice was almost back to normal. "I know, and Jordan? I'm sorry."

"Me too, Cara." The phone went dead in her ear, but she knew he had accepted her apology and things would still be okay between them.

She stared at the phone for a moment, unsure of what to do next and even more unsure of what to say about her emotional outburst. Cole was definitely getting to see her at her worst.

"David's dead." It was all she could think to say, and it summed everything up in two important words. What in the world was she supposed to do now? She had no idea who had hired David nor could she even question the man sent to silence him. She wasn't even positive David had been the one who killed Steve and knocked her out. Could there be more people involved in this? It was starting to feel much bigger than she had originally thought.

Cole tapped his fingers against the steering wheel for a moment. She was sure he had nothing to add, but then he spoke up. "Do you think his sister might have some knowledge?"

"What? The sister who has cancer? Why would she?"

"Don't you think if David was suddenly able to pay for cancer treatments that she might wonder where the money was coming from?"

Cara shrugged. She supposed it depended on how far along the cancer was and how close the siblings had been.

"It's at least worth a shot, right?"

"Yeah, I guess. Do you know where his sister lives?"

Cole flashed her a disarming smile. "What kind of criminal investigator would I be if I didn't?"

Once again, Cara felt her heart stutter in her chest. Not only did he not seem concerned about her outburst, but now he was smiling at her as if he was actually interested in her. Could he actually be interested in her? And if he was, what did she even do with that knowledge?

20

COLE

ole glanced over at Cara as the plane gathered speed on the runway. Her hands clutched the armrest on either side of her seat with a death grip that made her fingers look more like talons than fingers.

"Not a fan of flying?" She'd said nothing when he offered to purchase the tickets for the short flight to Vermont. They could have driven but the four-hour flight seemed preferable to a nearly twelve-hour drive. Nor had she said anything as they passed through the security check or waited in the boarding area. If she feared flying, any of those times would have been a better time to mention it than right before the plane left the runway.

She flashed him a tight smile. "Can't say it's my

favorite thing to do. In fact, I can't remember the last time I flew. I didn't even fly the first time I left Virginia."

Cole placed a hand on top of hers. "If you close your eyes and take a deep breath, it helps." He wasn't afraid of flying, but he'd once had a fear of public speaking, and this was one tactic his teacher had taught him.

Her eyes dropped to his hand before meeting his gaze again. She nodded and shut her eyes. Cole knew the fear of flying was common, but he had certainly not expected it from a woman as strong as Cara. She truly was like an onion. Every time he peeled away one layer, a different one lay beneath.

When the nose of the plane lifted and they were forced back into their seats, Cara's hand flipped over and gripped his. Her eyes didn't open but instead squeezed tighter. Cole smiled at the feeling of her skin against his. There certainly wasn't time for romance now, but he wondered if Cara would be open to it later. After the virus threat was mitigated.

It took until the plane leveled out for Cara to open her eyes. She looked at him before gently removing her hand. "I'm sorry. I shouldn't be afraid of flying."

Though he missed the warmth, he didn't try to grab her hand again. "It's understandable. Everyone has something they fear. My sister is an amateur kickboxer - tough as nails - but she's afraid of spiders."

He smiled as memories from his past flooded his mind.

"Once, she noticed a spider on the ceiling just before dinner. My father refused to kill it until after we'd eaten. She was so scared that she turned her chair around and ate with her back to us so she could keep the spider in her sights at all times." A soft chuckle escaped his lips as he pictured the scene again.

"How big was it?" Cara asked.

"What?"

"The spider? How big was it?"

Cole shook his head. "I don't even remember. Not too big I don't think."

"I can kill the small ones, but if they get bigger than a quarter…" She shook her head, a small smile pulling at the corners of her lips.

"Let me get this straight. You are a super tough military researcher and you're scared of flying and spiders?" He was teasing and he hoped she could tell by the lilt in his voice.

When she smacked his arm, he felt confident she did. "Okay, tough guy, what are you afraid of?"

"Me? Nothing." He shook his head but his smile remained.

"Oh, come on, you just said everyone is afraid of something, so what is it for you? Snakes? Scorpions? The dark?" The teasing lilt was now heavy in her voice.

"The dark? Really? Is that the best you got?"

Her eyes sparkled as she stared back at him.

"Women?" Her eyes widened as her mouth formed an "O" shape. "That's it, isn't it? You're afraid of women."

Cole chuckled. "If I were afraid of women, I wouldn't be here with you."

Cara shrugged. "I could be special. After all, I'm not like most women."

"No, you certainly aren't." The words left his lips before he could stop them, and even though he'd said them softly, he knew she'd heard them. They hung in the air like tantalizing treats just out of reach.

She bit her bottom lip, indecision burning in her eyes.

"Um, anyway," he continued in an effort to change the awkward subject. "I'm afraid of public speaking. That speech you gave about the virus a few days ago? I would have been sweating bullets."

She tilted her head and narrowed her eyes at him as if she didn't believe it. "But they were just friends."

He shook his head. "Doesn't matter. I can't even stand those small groups where everyone tells their name and a little about themselves. It's probably another reason I turned to criminal investigation. I rarely have to speak to more than one person at a time."

"I find that hard to believe," Cara said with a soft chuckle. "You were so good with the women at the church. Calm and cool. I wanted to be like you in that moment. People tell me I often come across as abrasive."

Cole would have used the word intimidating over abrasive, but he could see how people might say that about her. What he couldn't understand was his demeanor in front of the women. He should have been a stumbling mess, but Cara was right, he had been cool and collected. Had it been because the women were all grandmotherly? Or could Cara being by his side have had something to do with it?

"Perhaps we just make a good team."

She held his gaze a moment longer before agreeing. "Perhaps."

When the plane landed a few hours later, Cole stretched to ease his cramped back then rolled his neck a few times to loosen the stiffness. He waited until many of the passengers had de-boarded and then shook Cara's shoulder. She had fallen asleep about an hour into the flight, and he hadn't had the heart to wake her. He knew she hadn't been sleeping well, shouldering the guilt for everything that had happened.

"What?" She sat up, rubbing her eyes. "Have we landed already?"

"We have. You ready?"

She blinked a few times as her eyes adjusted to the light, ran a hand through her hair, and then nodded. "Yeah, let's go."

In the airport, she asked to stop at the restroom, and Cole took the time to check his appearance as well. Though his face was a little more haggard looking than he would have liked, he didn't have the dark circles Cara sported. He wished he'd brought a toothbrush though. Mints or gum on the way out would be a necessity. As well as some food. He hadn't had a good meal in hours.

Wetting his fingers slightly, he tousled his own hair, patted his cheeks to give them a little color, and then exited the bathroom to wait for Cara. She had apparently had the same idea as she appeared a little fresher as well. In fact, if he wasn't mistaken, she had applied a light gloss to her lips and a slight sparkle to her eyes. He bit back a smile. It appeared she had some girly tendencies after all.

"You mind if we grab some food before we head to the address? I'm famished."

She sent a smile in his direction. "Not at all. My stomach was protesting the lack of food as well a moment ago."

Though airport food was not always the best nor the cheapest, Cole didn't want to try to find a decent restaurant in an unfamiliar town. Instead, they settled on a chain restaurant they both agreed served good food.

"Tell me more about your family," Cara said after they had placed their order.

Cole leaned back and took a deep breath. He loved his family, but like every family, they had their quirks. Was he ready to share that with Cara?

"Well, I grew up in a small town in the South. My parents weren't farmers, but they lived out in the country on a large plot of land. It was pretty lonely growing up -

not many neighbors - so Cindy and I became close. She's two years younger than me. Blonde, perky, friendly. Pretty much everything I'm not."

Cara's brow furrowed. "I wouldn't say that. I think you're friendly. At least as long as you're not trying to arrest me."

Cole chuckled and pointed a finger at her in a "touché" gesture. "My mother was a teacher which was great on one hand because she was off summers with us, but she never let us slack on schoolwork."

"That's a good mother right there," Cara said as she lifted her water and took a sip. "How about your father?"

Cole bit the inside of his lip. His father was the chink in the perfect armor that was his family. It wasn't that his father was a bad guy, he just hadn't been there a lot. "My father was a broker. Investments. He spent most of his time at the office or studying stocks." He turned his water glass in a slow circle. "It's funny, I always said I didn't want to be like my dad. I wanted to help people and be there for my kids, but then I took a job where I work nearly as much as he did."

"You do help people though." Cara's voice was soft, and he saw the same caring attitude in her eyes.

"Yeah, I guess, but if I had kids, would my son think the same way about me that I thought about my dad? I think that's one reason I've been thinking of getting out and doing something else." He took a sip of his water and watched as Cara thought about what to say.

"Do you have kids now?"

Cole nearly spit his water out. "No."

"Close? I mean are you married? Engaged?"

Where was she going with this? "Not even dating."

"Well, then I think you have time to decide. You have time to choose if keeping people safe is more important than attending ball games or not. You have time to think of how you could do things differently than your dad. And you have time to think of how you could explain it to your son if you decide to stay with your job."

Cole felt the corners of his lips pull up in an irresistible smile. "You're something else, you know that?"

She dropped her eyes to the table and shook her head. "No, I'm just a woman who's seen a lot and has some big ideas."

There was something in the way she said those words that told Cole there was more to her background than getting teased for being overweight, but he could also tell she wouldn't be opening up about it right now. He filed the information away for later and opened his menu.

Cara couldn't keep her heart from racing as they stood in front of David's sister's house. Would Sarah be able to help them?

"I think it would be best if you let me do the talking at first," Cole said as he raised his hand to ring the bell. "I doubt she even knows of David's death yet."

Cara nodded. Though she'd never had to be the one to tell a family their loved one was dead, she had heard from friends in the military how hard it was.

It took a few moments before the door opened. A woman, thin and frail, stood on the other side. She didn't look much like David, but then Cara didn't look much like her sister either. "Are you two really sisters?" was a question she had heard so often growing up that it invaded her dreams for a time. In Sarah's case, the lack of resemblance could have also been due to her emaciated frame and balding head.

"Can I help you?"

"Yes ma'am. My name is Cole Davenport and this is my associate Cara Hunter. I'm a criminal investigator. Can you tell me if you are Sarah Grissom?" Cole flashed his badge and waited as the woman's eyes flicked from Cole to Cara and back again.

"I am, but I didn't call for a criminal investigator. What is this about?"

"It's about your brother David, actually."

Sarah's eyes widened and her grip on the door tightened. "Has something happened to David?"

Cole nodded. "I'm afraid he's been killed."

As Sarah's mouth dropped open, her knees folded and she began to sink to the floor. Cole rushed forward and propped an arm around the woman. "I know this is sudden news and we will answer any questions we can for you, but we really need to ask you about David as well. Would that be possible?"

Sarah nodded and opened the door wider to let them in. Cole kept his arm around the woman and helped her to a couch in the living room. Cara took a seat in one of the recliners that faced the couch. Though not elegant, the living room held a homey, comfortable feel as if secrets were often shared within it.

Sarah sat for a minute, her hand running absently up and down her arm. "How did he die?"

"That's what we need to talk to you about," Cole said as he sat in the other recliner. "David was admitted to the hospital with Melioidosis. Are you familiar with it?"

Cara watched Sarah closely as Cole spoke. While she probably wasn't as versed in spotting tells as he was, her gut was generally accurate when it came to judging people's character.

Sarah shook her head. "No, but it sounds like some sort of disease."

"It is," Cara said after Cole shot her a look that said she could explain. "It's a disease mainly found in tropical areas. I was studying it in order to try and create a vaccine."

"I don't understand then. How did David get it? He hasn't been anywhere tropical."

"Do you know how David was getting the money to pay for your cancer treatments?" Cole asked.

For a split second, Sarah's eyes grew larger and then her gaze slid to the side. Her hands twisted in her lap. "I don't know what you mean."

"Sarah, I'm fairly certain David stole my research and possibly killed my colleague. I met David briefly when he interned for my department, and I know he wasn't a bad guy. However, I'm afraid he got mixed up with some. David didn't die from the disease. Someone shot him while he was recovering in the hospital, and we need to figure out who before more people get hurt."

Sarah held her gaze for a moment before dropping her head into her hands. "I don't know who he was working for, but I guess I knew he was involved in something illegal. He told me that he had to. That it was the only way to afford the treatments. I told him we would find another way, but he was adamant."

"Did he ever mention a name? A group?" Cole asked, leaning forward.

Sarah shook her head. "I don't think so. All he ever said was that it was just one job. One job that would pay enough to cover all the treatments."

Disappointment flooded Cara as Sarah broke down. She'd known it was a long shot, but she'd been hoping Sarah would be able to tell them something, anything that would help her figure out who was behind all of this. Suddenly, the cufflinks jumped back into her mind. "Sarah, did David own cufflinks?"

Sarah sniffed and wiped at her eyes. "You mean the fancy things that go in buttonholes?"

"Yes, specifically gold ones with a snake emblem etched on them?"

Sarah shook her head. "No. I doubt he could have afforded them even if he had wanted them. Besides, he was afraid of snakes. He'd take on spiders or scorpions any day, but even little garter snakes freaked him out. There's no way he'd ever wear one."

Cara exchanged a look with Cole. If David didn't drop the cufflink, then who had? And why? Did that mean David hadn't killed Steve?

"Thank you, Ms. Grissom, for your time. We are so sorry for your loss." Cole stood and motioned for Cara to do the same. He pulled out a business card and placed it on the coffee table that sat in the middle of the room. "If you think of anything else, please don't hesitate to call me."

Through her tears, the woman nodded, and Cara and Cole took that as their leave to exit.

"I'm sorry that was a bust, Cole. We shouldn't have come all the way out here. Now it's late, and we'll never catch a flight back tonight."

He placed a hand on her arm. "Hey, first off, it was my idea to come out here, so there's no need for you to be sorry. Second, we learned that David probably wasn't the killer. Not unless he began liking snakes at some point in the last few months. Third, we were able to tell Sarah the news in person. Believe me, it's worse if you get news like that over the phone."

She looked at him, wondering when he'd gotten that phone call and whom it was about. It was obvious from his tone that he was speaking from experience. "I suppose you're right. I just wish I knew what to do next."

Cole checked his watch. "Well, it's just after eight. I

bet we could catch a Red-eye back to Fire Beach. It would make for a late night, but I'm game if you are."

Cara shrugged. "Might as well. There's no reason to stay here. I just wish there was more I could do back home. Without Steve's help, finding a vaccine will take years."

"What did your boss say about sending help?"

Cara rolled her eyes. "That he's working on it. Not too hard if you ask me."

"Maybe it's time to press him a little harder, see if we can get him to help in person."

Cara would love nothing more than for Malone to show up and take charge. She was a researcher, not a CDC specialist. Not that Malone was either, but he certainly had more experience with stuff like this than she did. "But what if he's in on it?"

Though she believed he was innocent, she hadn't been able to get Cole's words out of her mind since the moment he'd said them.

"Asking for it would be one way to find out, don't you think? Besides, what's that saying? Keep your friends close and your enemies closer."

Cara stared at him, a small smile pulling at her lips. "I bet you thought the same thing about me when you first came to Fire Beach."

Cole flashed a charming grin and shrugged. "It's possible."

"So where do I stand now?"

His eyes twinkled as he let go of her arm and walked toward the car. His words carried over his shoulder. "Guess you'll have to wait and see."

Cara smiled and shook her head before following him. She liked the fact that he could make her smile even in the midst of all the fear and chaos.

22

COLE

It was nearly five in the morning when the plane touched down back in Illinois. Cara had fallen asleep against Cole's shoulder, and he really didn't want to move her - he'd enjoyed the feel of a woman close to him again. However, before he could wake her gently, the lights did it for him as the plane came to a full stop and they switched on.

She opened her eyes and then jerked her head away as soon as she realized it had been resting against him. "Sorry, I didn't mean to fall asleep on you. I guess these late nights are taking a toll on me."

Cole certainly hadn't minded her head against him. In fact, he'd enjoyed the smell of her hair that tantalized his senses before he'd fallen asleep himself. "Completely understandable. In fact, when this is all over, I may have to find a place to pass out for a week."

"You and me both," she said as she pulled out her cell phone and turned it back on. Even though it was early in the morning, her phone began buzzing almost continuously with texts, missed calls, and voicemail notifications.

"Guess I've missed a few calls," she said with a slight chuckle. Her smile faded though as she scrolled through the log. "They're all from Nick. We better head to the hospital."

"Can we stop for a shower first?" The one thing Cole hated about flying was how sticky he always felt afterwards. Besides, sleep was still heavy on his shoulders but perhaps a hot shower and a cup of coffee would wake him up.

"Yeah, but we should make it a quick one. With this many calls, the news can't be good."

She was already returning Nick's call as they walked off the plane. Cole was glad they had parked at the airport and that they hadn't brought any luggage as it enabled them to get to the car faster. He heard only bits and pieces of Cara's discussion, but it certainly didn't sound like a pleasant one.

"Nick says all of the women from the church tested negative except one. However, they've had thirty people check themselves in who were in the pool. This is a disaster."

"I'll help in any way I can," Cole said, sending a quick glance in her direction as he pulled onto the interstate.

"I know. I just wish I had more researchers here, and I wish I knew for sure how to help the people in the hospital."

From the corner of his eye, Cole saw her hand tapping a nervous rhythm on her knee. Without taking his eyes from the road, he reached his right hand over and grabbed hers. She turned to look at him, but she did not pull her hand away. Instead, she laced her fingers through his and squeezed.

Cole felt his heart dance in his chest. How long had it been since a woman had made his heart do that? Years. Probably since Courtney in fact. When he'd gotten the call that she'd been killed by a drunk driver, he'd thought his heart would never thaw again. It had become a glacier of ice, driving him out of his original career as an advertiser and straight into the police academy. He'd told himself it was so he could stop crimes like that from hurting anyone else's loved ones, but he was becoming more certain he'd harbored a secret death wish.

Everyone knew police officers held a dangerous job, and he put himself in harm's way more often than not before he'd become a criminal investigator. Perhaps that was why his career in law enforcement had felt so unfulfilling. It wasn't what he was meant to do which begged the question, what was he supposed to do? Go back into advertising? Take a different path entirely?

The rest of the drive back to the bed and breakfast was quiet, but not uncomfortable. Makenna greeted them as they entered. She'd offered to help out until Cara could return to her post.

"I guess you heard the news," she said.

"Yeah, we're stopping long enough for a shower and coffee before we head over to the hospital. How bad is it?" Cara asked.

Makenna shook her head. "I'm not sure. Bubba just said he'd heard a lot of people had checked themselves in. Everyone's a little on edge."

Cole could see the guilt weighing on Cara's shoulders again. "Don't worry, Makenna, we'll figure this out."

She offered him a tight-lipped smile, and he headed to his room to clean up. Twenty minutes later, they were on the road again, feeling a little more refreshed and smelling a lot better.

The sun peeked over the hospital as they turned into the parking lot, but despite the beautiful colors lighting up the sky, Cara's face was somber.

"What if there's more bad news?" Her voice was little more than a whisper.

He turned the engine off and turned to face her. "That's possible, but I learned a long time ago that God is in control. All we can do is pray for the best outcome and trust that He knows best."

Cara nodded, though from the pained expression on her face, he wasn't sure his words had had the desired effect.

Nick greeted them at the nurses' station, his expression haggard and somber. "Did you find anything out from David's sister?"

Cole shook his head. "She suspected her brother was into something illegal, but she didn't know any specifics."

"Did he say anything before he was killed?" Cara asked.

Nick nodded and ran a hand across the back of his neck. "He did, but it wasn't much and it doesn't make sense to me. Again, he said he was sorry and then something about a snake." His hand scraped across the side of his neck before falling limply to his side.

Cole exchanged a glance with Cara. Again with the snake? Had David been referring to himself? Maybe he had taken on the symbol as a way to assuage the guilt he felt for the job he was doing. Or maybe he learned something about the man who was obsessed with the snake and that's what got him killed.

Cara swallowed and her voice was pinched when she spoke. "A snake? Like the slithering kind?"

Nick shrugged. "I don't know. He passed out again after that. His fever was still high though so he might have just been hallucinating, Cara."

"Yeah, maybe." Her finger tapped against her lips and Cole could tell her mind was running through the same possibilities his just had.

"Cara said you mentioned others. How are they doing?" Cole asked, turning the conversation back to the issue at hand. They could ruminate on what the snake meant later.

"Yeah. Jordan and the other officers managed to locate several people who had been at the pool. They're out looking again to see if they can reach the rest. We're still waiting on test results, but several of them have complained of pain or a cough. I'm hopeful that even if they are positive, we'll have reached them in time for treatment, but we did lose two."

Cara gasped and her hand flew to her mouth. "Two?"

Nick's hand found the back of his neck again. "Yeah, an elderly couple. Evidently, they had been at the pool a few days ago. Either they didn't realize they were running a fever or the disease hit them faster due to their weakened immune systems. Both had high blood pressure and diabetes which is the only explanation I can come up with for why it progressed quicker in them. Anyway, they never called anyone."

The blood drained from Cara's face. "You mean they died in their house?"

"They did."

"Oh my gosh. What if more people die like that?"

"That's why the cops are still out looking," Nick said. The pager on the waist of his pants began buzzing. He glanced down at it and then offered an apologetic smile. "I have to go, but I'll call if there's any new information here."

Cara nodded, but her head shook back and forth slightly. Suddenly, she whirled on Cole, the expression in her eyes harried and shocked. "I have to hold a press conference or get the news out to the media. We should have done that sooner. We've wasted so much time."

"Hey." Cole placed his hands on her arms to stop her spiral of blame. "We will. We'll go there next. It's going to be okay."

Tears glistened in Cara's eyes as she shook her head again. "It's not. It's not okay. How many more have to die because of me?"

He pulled her against his chest, his hand rubbing her back. "They didn't die because of you. You were trying to come up with a cure. Don't carry this burden."

Cara lifted her head. She wasn't much shorter than Cole and the movement brought her face inches from his. Cole's heart froze in his chest. He could feel her breath against his chin, see the gold flecks in Cara's eyes. Everything in his body wanted to kiss her, to see if her lips were as soft as they looked, but did she want that?

Her lips parted, and he held his breath. "We should get

to the media and then back to the research," she said, her words as soft as a butterfly's wings.

Cole fought against the desire raging through his body and swallowed his disappointment. "Right. Yes, let's go."

As he led the way back to the car, he couldn't help hoping there would be another moment like the one they'd just shared. A moment where he would not hesitate but would get to touch her lips with his own.

23

CARA

Cara fidgeted in her seat as the reporter, Melissa Beale, prepared everything for her interview. After hearing what she had to talk about, they had agreed to record the interview immediately and get it out on the next news show. Something Cara was immensely grateful for. In hindsight, she probably should have done this sooner, but she'd been hoping to avoid a city-wide panic. Now, she just hoped she could keep her composure in check. The sight of the lights and cameras was sending her heart into a thumping frenzy.

Her eyes slid to Cole who stood off to the side. She was glad he was here for moral support, but her head was still reeling from that almost kiss. What had that been about? Was he developing feelings for her or was that just a reaction to her stress? And if he was developing feelings for her, what did that mean?

There was no denying she found him attractive. Nor could she deny that her heart sped up a little every time he came close to her, but could she open her heart again? He certainly seemed different from her ex, but didn't they always?

"Ms. Hunter, are you ready?" Melissa asked.

Cara turned her attention back to the petite, perky woman with the perfect smile. She supposed a near perfect appearance was a requirement to be on television. She just hoped she didn't look too frumpy beside her. "Yes, of course."

"Wonderful. I'll do the opening. You just need to smile and wait for the questions."

Cara nodded. Smile and wait. She could do that. Hopefully her smile looked more natural than it felt.

There was an audible countdown followed by a moment of silence and then Melissa's face broke into a wide smile. "Hello, and welcome to a special segment of ANC News. I'm Melissa Beale and I'm joined today by Cara Hunter who owns one of the local bed and breakfasts in our area. Thank you for coming on today, Cara."

When she paused and lifted an eyebrow, Cara knew that was her cue to speak. "Thank you for having me, Melissa."

"Now, I'm sure all of the people in Fire Beach would

love to hear about your bed and breakfast, but that's not why you're here today, is it?" Another lift of the eyebrow.

"No, it's not. In addition to the bed and breakfast, I am also a medical researcher. It has been brought to our attention that someone has released a virus in our city." Cara swallowed hard and shifted in her seat.

"And you have information on where this virus was released?"

Cara nodded. "That is correct. I have been working with the Special Investigations Unit and we were able to determine that the virus was released into the community pool a few days ago and yesterday at the church garden. We are asking anyone who went swimming this week or who might have touched the food or soil in the garden to go into Fire Beach Hospital and get tested. This virus is very dangerous if left untreated."

"And what are the symptoms of this virus?" Melissa asked.

"Unfortunately, many, but the main ones are fever and pain. If you feel like you might have the flu, it is especially important that you get to the hospital immediately."

"This sounds serious. How scared should we be about this spreading from person to person?"

Cara shook her head. "It doesn't generally transmit that way thankfully. This disease spreads through soil, air, and water. We don't believe any of the virus was released into the air, but we aren't sure if there might be other places it

SECRETS AND SUSPENSE   157

was released. The most important thing is to get tested if you were at the pool or the garden and to monitor yourself and others for any flu like symptoms."

"Well, you've given us a lot to think about," Melissa said. "Thank you for coming on the show and sharing your knowledge with us."

"Thank you." Unsure what else to say, Cara glanced over at Cole. He shot her a thumbs up sign, making her smile slightly as Melissa wrapped up the interview. Before she knew it, the red lights of the camera had turned off and someone from the show was unclipping her microphone.

Melissa turned to her as she unclipped her own microphone. Her smile had faded, and her expression was somber. "How serious is this, Cara?"

"If people don't get treatment, it's very serious. Even with treatment, the morbidity rate is high. I'm on my way home to see if I can come up with a working vaccine, but the best thing to do would be to hope and pray that the person who started the spread didn't put it anywhere else."

As soon as the words came out of her mouth, Cara paused. She couldn't remember the last time she prayed, yet here she was telling a near stranger to do just that. Perhaps the saying that there were no atheists in fox holes was true. It was hard not to believe in God when you were faced with your own mortality.

She shook hands with Melissa, promising to return if

she had any new developments, before walking over to where Cole stood patiently waiting on the side.

"You did great out there. Looked very calm and professional."

"Thank you. I was nervous as all get out though." She took a deep breath and sighed. "Guess it's time to head back to the B&B and put my nose to the grindstone again."

Cole grinned and offered a mini bow. "Lead the way."

Cara tried to stifle her yawn as they pushed open the door to the outside. It had been a long few days, and the stress was really starting to weigh on her.

"Looks like you might need a nap when we get back to the house," Cole said as he opened his door.

"There's no time for a nap. If all of those people are sick, I have to find a vaccine that works or a way to make the cure more effective." This time she couldn't hold back the yawn that stretched her mouth as she inserted the key. She shot him a small smile. "But maybe I could use a large pot of coffee."

Cole returned the grin, his eyes twinkling. "I may not be much help with research, but I can definitely make some mean coffee."

Cara's smile remained until she pulled into her parking space. A very official looking black car with tinted windows sat in front of her B&B.

"Are you expecting company?" Cole's hand was already reaching inside his jacket for his gun as he spoke.

Cara shook her head. "Not unless Malone finally sent someone." She wished she had her gun on her as well, but she had forgotten to strap it back on after her hurried shower this morning.

"Stay behind me then," Cole said as he opened his door and stepped out first.

Cara stepped out next and made sure to walk toward the front of the car so she would be behind Cole as they made their way to the porch. They didn't make it that far before the doors of the black car opened and Malone, clad almost entirely in black, stepped out.

"Malone? What are you doing here?" She made no move to walk toward her boss, still unsure whether he could be trusted or not.

Malone's eyes shifted from her to Cole and back again. "I came to bring the help you requested. I was unaware you had found some."

Cara chuckled slightly. "Actually, this is Cole Davenport. He's a criminal investigator from Clarksville. He originally came to arrest me for Steve's murder, but I think I've managed to convince him I had nothing to do with that."

"Good. I would have vouched for you as well." Malone stumbled over his words as if caught off guard by the situation. "Anyway, I've been working on getting some help for you since the first time you called, and I've finally succeeded. I'm sure you were aware there were other teams researching other viruses as well?"

Cara was sure she had heard something along those lines a time or two before she and Steve had been forced to go undercover, but she'd never met any of them. Just like herself, they and their job didn't really exist on paper. "I've heard rumors."

Malone nodded as if this was the expected answer. Then he turned and opened the car door. A man in a brown plaid shirt and tweed pants stepped out followed by a woman with a nose ring and purple hair. The two could not have been more different. Had they been partners? Cara wondered what they could possibly find to talk about.

"Meet Anthony and Kat. They recently finished their research, and they have some time to help you with yours. That is if you have a place they can set up?"

Cara nodded. "Of course. I believe we have a few open rooms. Come inside."

Cole shot her a pointed look, but she shook her head slightly. Even if she didn't trust Malone completely, she didn't think the man would shoot her in the back in broad daylight. Still, it took all her resolve to turn her back on the people behind her and lead the way into the house.

Makenna looked up from the front desk as she entered. "Any news?" she asked, her voice fading as the others entered behind Cara.

Cara lifted an eyebrow, hoping that Makenna knew she

would explain later. "Thank you for watching the desk, Makenna. Can you help me get our guests checked in?"

"Um, absolutely." Makenna rolled back her shoulders and smiled brightly at the guests. "How many rooms will we be needing?" She was so convincing as an employee that Cara wondered if she'd ever done undercover operations.

"Four, if you have them."

Cara turned at Malone's voice. Four? It was only him and the two researchers, wasn't it? But no, standing beside Malone was Bruce, his bodyguard and driver. Of course, she should have known he would never come without Bruce. She'd often wondered if the man had military clearance or if he was an outside hire, but she'd never asked him.

"Okay, if I can just get a signature from everyone, I'll get your keys," Makenna said.

"It will all be going on my card," Malone said, stepping forward, "so I'll cover the cost."

"Absolutely, sir." Makenna kept up her professional demeanor, but Cara caught the slight hesitation. She was sure the woman was having a hard time not getting the identity of the other three people. Cara would have liked to have it as well, but what could she do?

As soon as Malone signed the form, Makenna turned to get the keys.

"I'll show everyone to their rooms. Thank you, Makenna." Cara took the keys and led the way to the rooms. She handed each key to the correct person as she showed them their room. "I'd like to grab another cup of coffee, but if you'd like to meet in the living room in half an hour, we can begin working."

Everyone nodded their agreement and Cara made her way to her room. What she really wanted was a nap, but now that Malone was here, she doubted she would be sleeping much at all.

❧ 24 ❧

COLE

"So, you want to tell me who all those people are?" Makenna asked Cole after Cara had taken the group away.

"I don't know much, but I'll tell you what I know. Not here though. Outside?" He jerked his head in the direction of the front door. Something about this group wasn't sitting right with him, and while he hoped it was just his mind running away with him, he didn't want to take any chances.

Makenna glanced over her shoulder and then around the room. Though they both knew no one was in the room, it was a police habit that was ingrained. "Yeah, the last guest checked out earlier, and if we stay out front, I'll see anyone who comes in."

As Cole closed the front door behind them, he felt the

weight lift from his shoulders slightly. They walked toward the mailbox to add a little more distance and give the illusion they were out to check the mail. "So, the guy who paid is Cara's boss in the military. She calls him Malone, but I don't know if that's his first or last name."

"It's his last. He signed the card Bradley Malone."

Cole nodded. "We're still trying to figure out if he's on our side or working for the enemy."

Makenna glanced around and then opened the mailbox. "What's the evidence?"

Cole shook his head. "Not much. He placed an intern with them who then got super nosy. Supposedly Malone fired him because Cara never saw him again. That intern turned out to be David Grissom, the man we believe unleashed the virus here. Malone also informed Cara there was a leak in the department which was why they were told to go undercover, and he is the only person that she knew of who knew where both Cara and Steve moved to."

As her eyes widened, Makenna let out a low whistle. "That might not be a lot of evidence, but it's certainly a hefty heaping of circumstantial evidence. Okay, and how about the other three?"

"The smaller man and the woman are supposedly researchers like Cara brought here by Malone to help her find a vaccine faster. Anthony and Kat, I think."

Makenna tucked a strand of dark hair behind her ears. "Okay, that's certainly plausible. How about the big guy?"

Cole bit the inside of his lip. It was the big guy who set his nerves on end the most. "I don't know who he is. Malone didn't introduce him though Cara seemed to know who he was. My best guess would be Malone's driver, maybe even bodyguard?"

"I'm guessing you didn't get warm fuzzies from them either?"

That was certainly putting it mildly. "It's only a feeling, but my gut is rarely wrong. Something just seems off."

"I agree. The question is what do we do about it?"

Cole wished he had those answers, but he wasn't a researcher. He knew little about infectious diseases. He'd come here to find out who killed Steve Steele, and he'd stayed because of Cara. Still, even though the majority of the evidence pointed to David, Cole wasn't sure he was Steve's killer either. The cufflinks still bothered him.

"I'm not sure how to help Cara at the moment, but how would you like to help me research Malone in there?"

A slight smile curled Makenna's lips. "I'd be happy to. You know it's funny? I came here with the thoughts of stepping down from my position at my police department and taking something lighter here, but I seem to be doing more work than I did back in Woodville."

Cole chuckled. He could definitely relate. It wasn't that his job was wine and cigars back home, but rarely was he racing around like he was now and never had he needed to race against time or a virus. "I hear you. Why were you thinking of stepping down, if you don't mind my asking?"

Cole was curious about Makenna, but he was also curious as to her motivations. He wondered if it were an experience similar to his.

A sappy smile took over Makenna's face. "Actually? For a man." She shook her head. "I never thought I would upend my life for a guy, but here I am."

The image of Cara's first briefing popped into Cole's mind. He vaguely remembered a large man sitting next to Makenna. "One of the firemen?"

Makenna's smile grew. "Yeah, Bubba. You know we're kind of like you and Cara."

"What do you mean?" Cole's words sounded defensive even to his ears, but he hadn't told anyone about his feelings for Cara.

"I mean when I first met Bubba, I thought he was my killer, but he ended up being the victim instead." Her lips twisted into a teasing smirk. "Maybe you'll fall for Cara like I did for Bubba."

"Hah. I don't know if I have time for a woman in my life." The lie came out easily as he had told himself it often enough over the last few years, but Makenna was not convinced. Neither was Cole for that matter.

She shook her head at him in a scolding manner. "I used to think that as well, but the love of a good man or woman is better than a fulfilling career I'm finding."

Cole needed to change the subject and fast before he found himself uttering words he wasn't sure he could back up yet. It had only been a few days, but Cara had wormed her way into his heart. "You might be right, but before I think about a romance, I kind of need to wrap up a murder and help keep a virus from decimating this town first."

"Agreed. So, let's go see what we can find out about Bradley Malone."

Cole hoped they would find something. He would hate for the killer to be Cara's boss, but knowing was definitely better than wondering.

25

CARA

Cara heard the front door open and glanced out of her room to see who it was. Surprise flooded her as she watched Cole and Makenna enter his room. As the door closed, a sting of jealousy shot through her body. What were they doing together in his room? Wasn't Makenna with Bubba?

She shook her head to clear the traitorous thoughts. She held no claim on Cole. Yes, there had been fireworks and a near kiss, but he hadn't explicitly said he was interested in her. Nor did she know if she was interested in dating him. Okay, that was a lie. She was definitely interested in dating him. If she could ever find a vaccine and stop whoever wanted this virus and IF he wanted to date her. Besides, there could be some completely innocent reason the two had gone into his room alone. None were coming to mind at the moment, but she was sure there had to be one.

"Looking for something?"

Cara jumped at the deep voice that had managed to sneak up on her. Her shoulder smacked into the doorframe sending a sharp pain down her arm. Rubbing the tender spot, she turned to see Bruce staring at her with a raised brow. How on earth did that mac truck of a man sneak up on her? She had to keep her attention focused on the problem at hand and not on Cole.

"I was just coming out to join everyone in the living room." She offered him a smile, but he did not return it. His gray eyes continued to bore into hers. Okay, perhaps she could just change the subject. "What are you doing out here? Was your room not acceptable?"

"The room is fine."

Cara blinked at him, waiting for more, but he said nothing further. He was definitely a man of few words. "Great. Well, then I guess I'll head to the living room." She locked her door behind her and listened for the click as she pulled it shut. She didn't know why, but Bruce standing so near her room gave her the creeps.

Laptop firmly gripped under her arm, she made her way to the living room. Bruce followed, sending shivers and the urge to run down her spine with every step. Relief flooded her when she spied Anthony and Kat already in the room, setting their laptops up.

"Shall we wait for Malone?" Cara asked as she sat in one of the vacant chairs. She was glad Anthony and Kat had chosen the couch leaving only single chairs in the room. There was no way she wanted Bruce invading her space any more than he already had.

"He had to run an errand," Bruce said, taking a position behind the couch where he could easily see both Anthony's and Kat's screens. "He said to start without him."

Cara narrowed her eyes at Bruce, but the man's poker face was unreadable. It was unlike Malone to just disappear, but the other two researchers didn't seem phased by the news. Perhaps this had become normal behavior for him in the last year. Cara tried not to make more out of it, but she couldn't help wondering where he would have gone in the middle of a pandemic.

"Okay, well, let me share the information from my cloud with you." Her fingers flew across the keys and within moments, she had delivered the information from her server to their screens as well. Bruce's ability to see the information unnerved her, but perhaps Malone had asked him to survey and take notes.

Silence descended on the room as everyone read over the information she and Steve had collected over the last few years.

"So, it appears there was some benefit to using auxotrophic amino acid synthesis mutant strain *B. mallei,*"

Anthony said as he glanced up at Cara and adjusted his glasses.

"Yes, we were able to run that test in the lab before we were forced into seclusion. Unfortunately, while there was some improvement in the mice, they rapidly deteriorated around day sixty, leading us to believe that would only buy time but not a true cure."

Kat looked up from her laptop and blinked a few times as if processing what she was going to say before the words left her bright purple lips. Not only did her lip color match her hair, but she had accented her eyes with a similar color. "Since the auxotrophic *B. mallei* mutant deficient in an iron active transport system appeared to work for the acute inhalation variety of Burkholderia but not the others, maybe we need to look not at vaccines, but at two or three different types of cures."

Cara let the information saturate her brain before forming her question. "You're saying that perhaps a vaccine will not be possible due to the different varieties, but we could work on a cure for the acute inhalation variety, the topical exposure variety, and the ingested variety?"

Kat nodded once. "I know that is a lot more work, but as it appears that none of the trials the two of you performed worked in all of the cases, yet some worked well in certain cases, it may be the only option."

"I suppose it's worth looking into," Cara said slowly, "although it won't allow for a vaccine to keep people from being exposed. Plus, it would require that doctors know exactly how the patient was exposed. That isn't always a possibility."

"No," Anthony added, "but it would improve the survival rate in cases where it is known."

Hope began to pulse inside Cara's veins. Could this be the answer? "Okay, how about we each take one variety and review the previous attempts that worked well with that variety? Then we can bring back the strongest information to the table and maybe we can take something solid to the hospital."

The other two nodded in agreement. Bruce, who had remained silent up until that point, fixed her with a steely gaze.

"How many are sick currently?"

Cara blinked at the blunt question. Why did that even matter? "I'm not sure. I haven't checked in with Nick since this morning, but there were two the last time I spoke to him at that point and at least thirty awaiting results. Plus the three who had already died."

"That just seems like a small number to be going through all this work." His blunt, matter-of-fact tone bothered her. Did he not realize how deadly this disease was?

"Would you have preferred the whole town was sick? Or perhaps just me?" She threw the last part in to see if his face would give anything away. Was he behind the unleashing of this disease?

His glare could have cut glass, but it revealed nothing of his internal motivations. "Of course not."

"Good because even one death is too many, and the mortality rate for this disease is rather high. The sooner we can find a vaccine, the better. So, if it's okay with you, I'm going to get to work."

She returned her gaze to Anthony and Kat. "I'll continue researching the pulmonary infection since it's what I was studying earlier. Anthony, why don't you take localized and disseminated infection while Kat takes the bloodstream infection?"

The two researchers looked at each other and nodded. "Sounds good."

As if Bruce had just been hanging around to see the research and the resulting conclusion, he now slipped away leaving Cara even more concerned about him. Why had Malone brought him? Could he be the snake David referred to? She still didn't know what David had meant by that or if they had even been coherent words. Perhaps he had only been hallucinating.

With a sigh, Cara closed her laptop and stood to return to her room. Though she was glad to finally have help and was optimistic they had a better handle on this disease, she still had no idea who had killed Steve and David, and that bothered her. Would she ever be able to answer that question?

26

COLE

Cole rubbed his eyes as he pushed back from the computer and stretched. He and Makenna had been researching Bradley Malone for over an hour, and they had found little to convict him. Cara hadn't been kidding when she said he was squeaky clean. The man had nothing on his record, not even a parking violation. He had been with the military for over twenty years, married for eighteen, and had two kids. Caleb was a junior and Breanna a freshman.

"Is it just me or is this guy too perfect?" Makenna asked.

With a sigh, Cole stood and paced around the room. He needed to get some blood flowing to get his brain working again. "It's not just you."

"I mean this guy appears to have it all - the nice house, the perfect family, the leading edge on men's fashions."

The words caught in Cole's brain, and he paused. "Men's fashions? What do you mean?"

Makenna shook her head. "He's just dressed from head to toe in half of these pictures. Dress shirt, perfect tie, cufflinks."

"Cufflinks?" Excitement flooded Cole. Was this the break in the case they had been looking for?

"Yeah, little gold ones, why?"

Cole rushed back to her side and scooted the laptop his direction. His eyes devoured the picture, focusing on the man's wrists. Sure enough, tiny gold circles sparkled from the camera's flash. He clicked the zoom button.

"Did I miss something?" Confusion filled Makenna's voice.

"Cara and I thought David killed her friend Steve and attacked her, but my lab tech found a gold cufflink at Steve's crime scene. A cufflink with the image of a snake on it. David's sister was adamant he never wore cufflinks and that he hated snakes." The image grew larger, but it was so grainy that Cole couldn't make out the shape. "Does that look like a snake to you?"

Makenna leaned closer and shook her head. "I can't make it out, but I bet the police here could enlarge it. Let's take it to Jordan."

"Good idea." Cole shut the laptop and tucked it under his arm. "Should we tell Cara?"

"Let's wait until we know for sure. She's probably deep into research right now."

Cole had no doubt that was the truth. Cara had a laser-like focus on whatever she was working on and disturbing her would only delay her finding a vaccine. Besides, Makenna was right. Cole would hate to get Cara's hopes up only to disappoint her again. "You're right. Let's go."

Twenty minutes later, Cole followed Makenna into the Fire Beach police department.

"Can you page Jordan Graves for us?" Makenna asked the sergeant at the desk. Her gray hair hung in a chin-length bob, and no makeup adorned her face which seemed permanently fixed in a serious expression.

"What would you like me to tell him it's about?"

"Could you just tell him that Makenna and Cole are here and we need his help?"

Sergeant Serious lifted a single brow, but picked up the phone. "Detective Graves? You have two visitors here who say they need your help."

A minute later, Jordan, stoic as ever, appeared before them. "What's going on? Did you find something out?"

"Possibly," Cole said, stepping forward and indicating the laptop under his arm. "Do you have the ability to enhance a photo?"

Jordan nodded and led the way to their crime lab. After

pulling up the photo on their machine, he began zooming in.

"The cufflinks." Makenna pointed impatiently at that part of the picture. "Zoom in on the cufflinks."

After a few more clicks, the image cleared, and Cole sucked in his breath. It was a perfect match to the cufflink Wendy had found at Steve's crime scene which meant one of two things. Either Bradley Malone had also been at Steve's place or he had killed Steve. Had he also been the one to attack Cara as well?

"Does somebody want to tell me why this is important?" Jordan looked from Makenna to Cole.

"A cuff link that looked exactly like this was found at Steve Steele's crime scene, and that cuff belongs to Cara's boss."

Jordan's eyes widened with alarm. "Does Cara know? We have to tell her."

"I'll call her now." Cole pulled out his phone and stepped away as he dialed Cara's number. The phone rang in his ear once, twice... "Come on, Cara, pick up." The ringing stopped and relief flooded him, but it lasted only a moment as her voicemail kicked on.

Ending the call, he walked back to Jordan and Makenna. "We have a problem. Cara's not picking up."

27

CARA

Cara couldn't believe she was tailing Bruce. This was bound to be a bad idea. Every fiber of her being screamed out that she should have taken Cole with her or that she should call Jordan, but tell them what? Perhaps the man was just going for coffee or to grab something from the store. She would call them as soon as she knew for sure.

Bruce pulled into the parking lot of a large warehouse. Cara wasn't immediately familiar with the building, but she knew following him into the lot would give her away. She drove slowly past the entrance and pulled into a building across the street. Turning off her car, she watched as Bruce got out of his car, looked around, and then headed into the building. This was no coffee shop, but what was this building?

Craning her neck, she scanned the building for any signs that would allow her to see what it was, but there was nothing. It was large, bare, and...

The knock at her window sent her heart thundering in her chest, but before she could react, the door opened and Malone's face appeared. "Cara, so happy you could stop by. Why don't you join me?"

Cara bit her lip as she quickly considered her options. She could reach for her phone but Malone would get her before she could dial 9-1-1. It would be better to leave it in the car and hope someone pinged her cell when they realized she was missing. Surely Cole or Makenna would come looking for her soon.

The knife she always kept strapped to her ankle was there, but she didn't want to give it away yet. She needed to be sure Malone was an enemy before she attacked him. Otherwise, she would be spending time in prison which was definitely not her goal. No, better to just go with him and let it play out.

"Sure, Malone, but I wasn't expecting to see you here." She flashed up what she hoped was a confident smile before stepping out of the car to join him.

"Really? You followed my bodyguard here. I can't imagine you didn't think I'd be nearby." Though he still looked the same, there was an unnatural edge to his voice that Cara had never heard before. He withdrew a gun and motioned for her to walk toward the warehouse.

Her mouth dried up as she began the walk she was fairly certain would lead to her death. "Why did you take Bruce here?" A thousand scenarios ran through her mind - none of them good - but she wanted to hear it from Malone's mouth.

"I bring Bruce everywhere. He's quite handy to have around for protection and to clean up messes."

"You mean messes like David?" She paused and glanced his direction

A momentary look of ire flashed across his face before he composed himself again. "David was incompetent. He was supposed to secure the research and the samples and tie up the loose ends, but he failed miserably."

"Loose ends like Steve and myself?" Though she was still guessing, the pieces were beginning to fall into place for Cara and they were not painting a happy future.

"The barrel of the gun poked her back. "Neither of you were supposed to survive, but David didn't have the courage to finish the job. While he got the research and the samples, Steve called me as soon as he came to, and I had to finish the job. Bruce was supposed to make sure you were taken care of, but the arrival of your friends interrupted his mission."

"Didn't have the stomach to finish me yourself?" Cara shot at him. Feelings of anger and betrayal simmered beneath her skin.

Malone shrugged. "I always had a soft spot for you. I could have done it, but I wouldn't have enjoyed it."

"And you enjoyed killing Steve? We trusted you. Why would you kill him?"

"Money, Cara. I needed money."

"Money?" She nearly choked on the word. Steve had been killed for money?

They reached the door of the warehouse and Malone pulled it open. "High school is expensive, Cara. Caleb is playing football which is several thousand dollars and Brianna does gymnastics and now cheer. You know how little the military pays. I needed money to afford life. Some very interested buyers found out about our research and offered a nice sum of money in return for access to the virus."

"Terrorists, you mean. What if they unleash it on the U.S.?" The door opened to a dimly lit hallway, and Cara struggled to see in front of her.

"That's why I had to wait until you were close to a vaccine. Well, I guess a cure in this case. Steve probably would have told you at your meeting, but he had just discovered the day before what you three did this afternoon. One vaccine won't work, but three different treatments will. Now that we have that information, I can relax and deliver the goods to my buyers."

"Do you even have any left? Didn't David use it all to infect the pool and the garden?"

"You think David did that?" A dark laugh billowed out of Malone's throat. "We poisoned the pool and then injected David directly. Once his fever spiked, then we gave him the watering can and dropped him off at the church."

Cara stopped once again and turned to Malone. "Then why kill him in the hospital?"

Malone shook his head. "Because I know how good you are. When you called and told me you knew who he was, I knew you would have already put him on medication. I couldn't take the chance he would wake up and tell you anything. It was a shame to lose Charles, but I couldn't send Bruce in case the cops were called." He poked her again with the gun. "Walk."

The whole picture was now clear for Cara, all but one question. "How did David get involved in all of this anyhow?"

"He came to me a year ago asking for a job. I'm sure you know his sister has cancer, and he couldn't afford treatments. He was supposed to just report to me what the two of you were discovering, but he got antsy and I had to get rid of him. Fortunately for him, he had excellent computer skills. The computers at the base were impenetrable, but he assured me he could hack into your private servers if I could get the two of you off base."

Cara felt sick to her stomach. How had Malone fooled her so easily? Perhaps she had been distracted by her breakup with Stan. No, if she was honest, she knew she hadn't been at the top of her game since she'd met Stan. That was evidenced by the fact that she had let him abuse her for so long.

The hallway opened to a large room where several men stood around talking. Bruce turned as they approached and flashed a large smile. "I told you she wouldn't be able to resist following me, Boss." He picked up a rope from a table as he walked their direction.

"You did well, Bruce. This will certainly be easier to explain than killing her in her bed and breakfast." Malone shoved her into a chair and Cara immediately felt rope burn into the sensitive skin of her wrist. She prayed Bruce would not feel the knife when he tied up her ankles.

Suddenly Malone's face was in front of hers. "Now I have a question for you, Ms. Hunter. What tipped you off?"

Again Cara ran through her options. He obviously didn't know about the cufflink and telling him might make him speed up whatever his plan was, so she kept that information to herself. Instead, she shrugged. "A lot of things, actually, but mostly the fact that you knew where Steve and I were and missing the meeting an hour ago seemed uncharacteristic for you."

"Ah, yes, I knew I was taking a risk doing that, but it was unavoidable. I am sorry it has to come to this, Cara, but if you'll excuse me, I have to finish up this transaction and get back to Virginia. I've been gone too long as it is."

Malone joined the other men who appeared of Arabian descent and disappeared through another doorway leaving her alone with Bruce. Cara closed her eyes and did something she hadn't done in a long time. She prayed.

28

COLE

"Al, ping Cara's phone. She may not be answering, but she never goes anywhere without it. Hopefully, it will show her location. Albright, call the B&B and see if anyone's seen her. Givens, get me anything you can on Bradley Malone. I want to know if he owns any businesses out here." Jordan began barking out orders as soon as Cole delivered the information that he couldn't get Cara on the phone.

Stone entered from his office and Jordan updated him on the intel. "Have we identified the shooter from the hospital yet?" Stone added after he was caught up.

"Not yet, sir," Al spoke up, "but I've got Cara's phone. It's at the old heating and cooling warehouse on Wabash Avenue."

"All right, let's suit up. Givens, I want you to stay and

keep looking into Malone. I want more than a cufflink to pin on him, especially considering he's military."

Makenna stepped forward. "I know we haven't met sir, but my name is Captain Drake of the Woodville police department. What can I do to help?"

Stone looked her over for a moment as if deciding if he could trust her. "Stay with Givens. I want the ID on the shooter. Hopefully, we can link the two."

His eyes turned to Cole, and Cole stepped forward. "Cole Davenport, sir. Criminal investigator for Clarksville. I'd like to come."

"Absolutely not," Stone roared. "This team is highly trained. Inexperience is dangerous."

Cole clenched his jaw. There was no way he was sitting this out. If Cara was in trouble, he was going to be there.

As if sensing his thoughts, Jordan stepped forward. "Captain, he's been helping Cara with this case from the beginning. Plus, he's met Malone and a few of the other players. It might be a good idea to bring him along."

Stone's expression grew even fiercer if that was possible, but after exchanging a glare with Jordan, he let out a sigh and relented. "Fine, but he stays at the back and follows orders." He shot the last two words directly at Cole who nodded. He didn't care what orders he had to follow as long as he was there to help save Cara.

Twenty minutes later, Cole adjusted his bulletproof

vest as he stepped out of the car and joined Jordan and the others.

This time Al took the lead. "Okay, there are two entrances to the warehouse." She tapped on her cell phone and Cole leaned closer to Jordan to see the schematics they all had on their phones.

"Al and Jordan, you take Cole and enter at this closest entrance," Stone said. "Albright and I will go around the other side to head them off. Now, we don't expect there are any innocents besides Cara inside, but keep your wits about you. Flash bangs as much as possible. Let's try to keep the body count down and bring these guys to justice."

The men and Al nodded and then Stone and Albright jogged out of sight. Jordan turned to Cole. "You ready for this?"

Not in the least, but there was no way Cole was saying that out loud. His throat was parched, and his heartbeat thudded in his ears, but he nodded. He and Cara were not officially involved, but there was no way he was waiting outside and getting the news - good or bad - second hand. He gave Jordan a curt nod and fell into step behind him.

Al took the lead, and after scouting the area for cameras, she opened the door and stepped inside. It took a few blinks for Cole's eyes to adjust to the light. They were in a dimly lit hallway. He pulled his gun, enjoying the heavy feeling in his hand. It was just a weapon and no guarantee of survival, but it had saved him more than once.

The building was quiet as they made their way down the hallway. Cole hoped they weren't too late. Visions of Cara's dead body floated across his mind and he squeezed his eyes shut to remove them. "God, please let her be okay," he whispered softly.

Light appeared ahead of them and Al paused. She held up a hand for them to stop as she scoped around the corner. Cole held his breath as he waited.

"I see Cara," she whispered. "She's tied up to a chair and some large guy is guarding her."

"That's probably Malone's driver. I'm fairly certain he's also his bodyguard." Cole was glad he was able to supply some helpful information.

"Okay, I'll throw a flashbang. Jordan and I will run in first to neutralize the driver and anyone else who might be around. You get Cara."

Cole nodded and stepped behind Jordan. Al threw the flashbang. There was a loud noise followed by a bright flash of light and then chaos ensued. Gunshots sounded, but unconcerned for his own safety, Cole followed Al and Jordan into the larger room. The acrid smell of smoke burned his throat and stung his eyes, but he made his way over to Cara who was still very much alive.

"Malone's in the other room with the terrorists. They still have some of the virus."

"Stone and Albright came in the other way. I'm sure they'll find them," Cole said as he holstered his gun and pulled out a knife to cut her ropes. When she was free, he grabbed her hand and pulled her toward the entrance.

She dug her heels in, halting their escape. "We have to help them."

Cole turned to her and found her eyes. There was no time for this, but he knew he would have to say it to get her to leave. "You aren't armed, and I'm not losing you. They've got this. Now, come on."

A flood of emotions crossed over her face, but a smile won out in the end. "You can't lose me?"

Cole returned the smile and shook his head. Of course that's what she focused on. "Can we talk about this later? Like maybe when we aren't in danger of getting shot?"

Her eyes twinkled, but she squeezed his hand and ran with him out of the building. Cole didn't stop until they were back to the cars. He had no idea how long Jordan and the others would take, but he felt this was at least a safe enough distance from the warehouse that they could stop for a minute.

He turned Cara to face him and placed his hands on her cheek. "You stubborn woman. Why did you come here alone?" Anger at the actions that had put her in danger conflicted with the relief he felt that she was okay.

Her eyes widened and filled with emotion. "I'm sorry. I was just going to follow Bruce to see if I could find anything out. I didn't know he was leading me into a trap. How did you even find me?"

"Makenna and I did some research on Malone and found pictures of him wearing the cufflinks. I tried to call and warn you, but when you didn't pick up, I knew you were in trouble. Al pinged your phone, and the rest is history." He ran his thumb across her cheek as if to assure himself she was real and safe.

"I can't believe Stone let you come." Her words were quiet and breathy, and her eyes bored into his soul.

"There was no way I was staying, Cara." His husky tone declared his desire to kiss her, but he didn't care. She was alive, she was in his arms, and if he had his way, that's where she would be staying in the future.

"Because you couldn't lose me?"

It was a question, but not one that needed a verbal answer. Her gaze fell to his lips, and he knew that the truest way to convince her of his feelings would be with actions and not words. As his lips pressed against hers, she leaned toward him. Her hands pulled at his hair as her body melded into his.

The wall that had been so carefully constructed around his heart after his fiancée was killed exploded into a million pieces. It had been years since he had considered letting love in again, but in less than a week, Cara had ignited the fuse and the desire burned within him now.

"Ahem." A throat cleared behind them and reluctantly Cole pulled away from Cara.

"Sorry to interrupt you two." A light pink colored

Jordan's cheek and he appeared unable to look either of them in the eyes. "We've apprehended Malone and three other men. Stone and Albright are clearing the building, but I wanted to make sure you both had gotten out all right. I see that you have."

Cara stepped forward and threw her arms around her embarrassed friend. "Thank you for coming for me, Jordan. For everything, really."

He nodded. "I'll call for backup to help with transport. Why don't you take my car and go back to the B&B.? You could both use a little rest."

"Not yet," Cara said, shaking her head. "I need to get to the hospital and let Nick know what I found out. I'm sure it will help him cure the rest of the patients."

"And we should probably check on Makenna," Cole added.

Jordan shook his head. "I'll take care of Makenna. You stop at the hospital and then rest. That's an order."

"Yes sir." As she popped a salute, a wide smile filled Cara's face and Cole thought she had never looked more beautiful. He decided he would do whatever it took to make sure that smile remained.

THE EPILOGUE
CARA

"Do I have to do this?" Cole asked as he tucked his green button-down shirt in.

Cara smiled as she turned from the mirror she had been checking her makeup in and crossed to him. She loved the green color on him. It brought out the green flecks in his brown eyes. "It's just a small party." She placed her hands on his chest and brushed a speck of lint from the right side. "Ginny hasn't celebrated her birthday in years, so this is important to her."

He rolled his eyes good-naturedly. "I know."

Actually, he didn't. He'd never dated an abuser, but Cara had, and she'd slowly told him about her last relationship over the past few days. She appreciated that he was trying to understand.

Ginny had overcome an even worse experience. She'd come to Fire Beach a little over a month ago after getting the courage to leave her abusive boyfriend. He hadn't allowed her to work or celebrate in years, but Cara and her friends had accepted Ginny into their fold. She now worked at Fire Dreams and was dating Jordan's brother, Graham.

Cara returned her hands to rest on Cole's muscular chest and flashed a teasing grin up at him. "Besides, we have a lot to celebrate, don't you think?"

The last week had been a whirlwind and one Cara was glad was over. The information she had given Nick had allowed him to administer an effective treatment for the people who had been infected at the pool. Everyone, including little Robbie, had recovered, and Malone, Bruce, and the terrorists were now behind bars. The remaining samples of the virus had been collected and returned to the military where they were placed under lock and key.

Due to her work, the military had agreed to allow Cara to finish her remaining contract in Fire Beach, and Cole had turned in his notice. He would have to go back for another few weeks to pack and get everything situated, but he was planning on making Fire Beach his new home. While he wasn't sure what he wanted to do yet, Cara knew that with his background in advertising that he could find a job in town.

He wound his arms around her waist and pulled her closer. "The only thing I need to celebrate is finding you."

As he placed a soft kiss on her lips, she thought of how lucky she was, how lucky they both were. She had never thought she deserved a good man - having been put down by her father and others growing up. He had lost the woman he'd planned to marry to a drunk driver. They were both damaged, but God had brought them together to find healing. She had never believed in love developing so quickly, but as the thought of losing Cole tore her to pieces, she knew she was there.

Summoning all her resolve, she gently pulled back, breaking the kiss. "Come on, we have to go or we're going to be late. We can continue this later."

Cole let out a reluctant sigh, but the twinkling in his eyes told her he wasn't really upset. "I'm going to hold you to that, Ms. Hunter."

Smiling, Cara shook her head and led the way out to the car.

A few minutes later, they pulled into the nearly full parking lot of Fire Dreams. Jordan and Graham had closed the restaurant early for Ginny's private party, but as their group of friends seemed to keep growing, it didn't surprise her to see so many cars.

She pulled into an empty spot and turned off the car. After grabbing Ginny's present and locking the car, she took Cole's hand and smiled up at him. "Are you ready for this?"

Though he'd been spending as much time as he could in Fire Beach the last few weeks, most of these people were still mostly strangers to him. She knew how hard it was for him to loosen up around people he didn't know well.

"Just don't leave me alone, and I'll be fine." He gave her hand a gentle squeeze and pulled the door open.

Lively conversation carried out as soon as they stepped inside. The corners of Cara's lips pulled up as she took in the group. Ginny and Graham sat at the head of the table. Jordan and Cassidy were next to them followed by Bubba and Makenna. Across from Jordan and Cassidy were Tia and Brody. Nick, Ivy, and Al rounded out the group leaving just two spaces for her and Cole. Jordan and Graham had already had to pull three tables together to accommodate everyone. If they got any bigger, and Cara had no doubt they would, they would need to add a fourth table.

Cole's grip on her hand tightened as she led the way toward Ginny. "Happy belated birthday, friend." Cara held out the present and surrendered when Ginny threw her arms around her.

"Thank you, Cara. I'm so glad you guys could make it." She turned to Cole. "I know I don't know you well, but

I hear that you're staying in town, so hopefully we can remedy that."

"Uh, yeah sure," Cole said with only a slight stutter.

Cara had never seen Ginny so excited, but after hearing about her past, she could understand why. The girl had a lot of missed celebrations to catch up on. After handing off the gift, Cara and Cole took their seats - Cole next to Makenna and Cara next to Al.

Cara wondered what Al's story was. She didn't know the female officer well, but she was pretty with her blonde hair and ski-sloped nose. Plus, Cara knew she was loyal to a fault. She had heard enough stories about her from Jordan to know that. Cara had no doubt a romance was in Al's future. Perhaps with Nick? Her eyes flicked between the two of them, but she couldn't really picture them together.

Al's phone buzzed on the table, and she picked it up. Cara had assumed she was going to silence it as the party was just beginning to get started, but instead her eyes widened and her mouth fell open.

Cara leaned over to whisper, "Are you okay?"

Al shook her head. "That was my mom. My sister is missing."

The End!

. . .

IF YOU LIKED THIS STORY, PLEASE LEAVE A REVIEW. JUST A few words really helps!

Want to find out what happened to Al's sister? Be sure to read Rescue My Heart coming soon and if you want to know more about Ginny's story, be sure to read Love on the Run.

IT'S NOT QUITE THE END!

Thank you so much for reading *Secrets and Suspense*. As I said in the beginning, this was a hard book to write as when I got to it, I was living through an outbreak and it wasn't fun. However, I like the way this ended up, and I think it stayed true to my intention. I love the characters of Fire Beach, and I always enjoy developing them more. I hope you enjoyed learning about Cara and meeting Cole. If you did, would you do me a favor and please leave a review? It really helps. It doesn't have to be long - just a few words to help other readers know what they're getting.

I'd love to hear from you, not only about this story, but about the characters or stories you'd like read in the future. I'm always looking for new ideas and if I use one of your characters or stories, I'll send you a free ebook and paperback of the book with a special dedication. Write to me at loranahoopes@gmail.com. And if you'd like to see what's coming next, be sure to stop by authorloranahoopes.com

I also have a weekly newsletter that contains many wonderful things like pictures of my adorable children, chances to win awesome prizes, new releases and sales I might be holding, great books from other authors, and anything else that strikes my fancy and that I think you would enjoy. I'll even send you the first chapter of my newest (maybe not even released yet) book if you'd like to sign up.

Even better, I solemnly swear to only send out one newsletter a week (usually on Tuesday unless life gets in the way which with three kids it usually does). I will not spam you, sell your email address to solicitors or anyone else, or any of those other terrible things.

God Bless,
      Lorana

❦ 29 ❦

NOT READY TO SAY GOODBYE
YET?

ME EITHER, BUT I DO HAVE A FEW OTHER BOOKS I HAVE TO write before I come back to Fire Beach. In the next book, we'll see what happened to Al's sister and of course meet a handsome new leading man. Be sure to order your copy today of Rescue My Heart!

Rescue My Heart

How do you save someone who doesn't want to be saved?

Detective Al Parker's sister has gone missing, but when Al finds out where she's gone, will she be able to save her? And who is the man she runs into? Friend or foe?

Find out in this gripping romantic suspense by best-selling author Lorana Hoopes. Fans of Alana Terry, Susan May Warren, and Margaret Daly will love this spine-tingling ride.

ॐ 30 ॐ

A FREE STORY FOR YOU

Enjoyed this story? Not ready to quit reading yet? If you sign up for my newsletter, you will receive The Billionaire's Impromptu Bet right away as my thank you gift for choosing to hang out with me.

The Billionaire's Impromptu Bet

A SWAT officer. A bored billionaire heiress. A bet that could change everything….

Read on for a taste of The Billionaire's Impromptu Bet….

THE BILLIONAIRE'S IMPROMPTU BET PREVIEW

Brie Carter fell back spread eagle on her queen-sized canopy bed sending her blond hair fanning out behind her. With a large sigh, she uttered, "I'm bored."

"How can you be bored? You have like millions of dollars." Her friend, Ariel, plopped down in a seated position on the bed beside her and flicked her raven hair off her shoulder. "You want to go shopping? I hear Tiffany's is having a special right now."

Brie rolled her eyes. Shopping? Where was the excitement in that? With her three platinum cards, she could go shopping whenever she wanted. "No, I'm bored with shopping too. I have everything. I want to do something exciting. Something we don't normally do."

Brie enjoyed being rich. She loved the unlimited credit

cards at her disposal, the constant apparel of new clothes, and of course the penthouse apartment her father paid for, but lately, she longed for something more fulfilling.

Ariel's hazel eyes widened. "I know. There's a new bar down on Franklin Street. Why don't we go play a little game?"

Brie sat up, intrigued at the secrecy and the twinkle in Ariel's eyes. "What kind of game?"

"A betting game. You let me pick out any man in the place. Then you try to get him to propose to you."

Brie wrinkled her nose. "But I don't want to get married." She loved her freedom and didn't want to share her penthouse with anyone, especially some man.

"You don't marry him, silly. You just get him to propose."

Brie bit her lip as she thought. It had been awhile since her last relationship and having a man dote on her for a month might be interesting, but.... "I don't know. It doesn't seem very nice."

"How about I sweeten the pot? If you win, I'll set you up on a date with my brother."

Brie cocked her head. Was she serious? The only thing Brie couldn't seem to buy in the world was the affection of Ariel's very handsome, very wealthy, brother. He was a movie star, just the kind of person Brie could consider marrying in the future. She'd had a crush on him as long as she and Ariel had been friends, but he'd always seen her as just that, his little sister's friend. "I thought you didn't want me dating your brother."

"I don't." Ariel shrugged. "But he's between girl-friends right now, and I know you've wanted it for ages. If you win this bet, I'll set you up. I can't guarantee any more than one date though. The rest will be up to you."

Brie wasn't worried about that. Charm she possessed in abundance. She simply needed some alone time with him, and she was certain she'd be able to convince him they were meant to be together. "All right. You've got a deal."

Ariel smiled. "Perfect. Let's get you changed then and see who the lucky man will be.

A tiny tug pulled on Brie's heart that this still wasn't right, but she dismissed it. This was simply a means to an end, and he'd never have to know.

JESSE CALHOUN RELAXED AS THE RHYTHMIC THUDDING OF the speed bag reached his ears. Though he loved his job, it was stressful being the SWAT sniper. He hated having to take human lives and today had been especially rough. The team had been called out to a drug bust, and Jesse was forced to return fire at three hostiles. He didn't care that they fired at his team and himself first. Taking a life was always hard, and every one of them haunted his dreams.

"You gonna bust that one too?" His co-worker Brendan

appeared by his side. Brendan was the opposite of Jesse in nearly every way. Where Jesse's hair was a dark copper, Brendan's was nearly black. Jesse sported paler skin and a dusting of freckles across his nose, but Brendan's skin was naturally dark and freckle free.

Jesse flashed a crooked grin, but kept his eyes on the small, swinging black bag. The speed bag was his way to release, but a few times he had started hitting while still too keyed up and he had ruptured the bag. Okay, five times, but who was counting really? Besides, it was a better way to calm his nerves than other things he could choose. Drinking, fights, gambling, women.

"Nah, I think this one will last a little longer." His shoulders began to burn, and he gave the bag another few punches for good measure before dropping his arms and letting it swing to a stop. "See? It lives to be hit at least another day." Every once in a while, Jesse missed training the way he used to. Before he joined the force, he had been an amateur boxer, on his way to being a pro, but a shoulder injury had delayed his training and forced him to consider something else. It had eventually healed, but by then he had lost his edge.

"Hey, why don't you come drink with us?" Brendan clapped a hand on Jesse's shoulder as they headed into the locker room.

"You know I don't drink." Jesse often felt like the outsider of the team. While half of the six-man team was married, the other half found solace in empty bottles and meaningless relationships. Jesse understood that - their job was such that they never knew if they would come home night after night - but he still couldn't partake.

Brendan opened his locker and pulled out a clean shirt. He peeled off his current one and added deodorant before tugging on the new one. "You don't have to drink. Look, I won't drink either. Just come and hang out with us. You have no one waiting for you at home."

That wasn't entirely true. Jesse had Bugsy, his Boston Terrier, but he understood Brendan's point. Most days, Jesse went home, fed Bugsy, made dinner, and fell asleep watching TV on the couch. It wasn't much of a life. "All right, I'll go, but I'm not drinking."

Brendan's lips pulled back to reveal his perfectly white teeth. He bragged about them, but Jesse knew they were veneers. "That's the spirit. Hurry up and change. We don't want to leave the rest of the team waiting."

"Is everyone coming?" Jesse pulled out his shower necessities. Brendan might feel comfortable going out with just a new application of deodorant, but Jesse needed to wash more than just dirt and sweat off. He needed to wash the sound of the bullets and the sight of lifeless bodies from his mind.

"Yeah, Pat's wife is pregnant again and demanding some crazy food concoctions. Pat agreed to pick them up if she let him have an hour. Cam and Jared's wives are having a girls' night, so the whole gang can be together. It will be nice to hang out when we aren't worried about being shot at."

"Fine. Give me ten minutes. Unlike you, I like to clean up before I go out."

Brendan smirked. "I've never had any complaints. Besides, do you know how long it takes me to get my hair like this?"

Jesse shook his head as he walked into the shower, but he knew it was true. Brendan had rugged good looks and muscles to match. He rarely had a hard time finding a woman. Jesse on the other hand hadn't dated anyone in the last few months. It wasn't that he hadn't been looking, but he was quieter than his teammates. And he wasn't looking for right now. He was looking for forever. He just hadn't found it yet.

Click here to continue reading The Billionaire's Impromptu Bet.

DISCUSSION QUESTIONS

1. What was your favorite scene in the book? What made it your favorite?

2. Did you have a favorite line in the book? What do you think made it so memorable?

3. Who was your favorite character in the book and why?

4. What was the hardest part of dealing with the Covid-19 virus for you?

5. What did you learn about God from reading this book?

6. How can you use that knowledge in your life from now on?

7. What do you think would make the story even better?

THE STORY DOESN'T END!

You've met a few people and fallen in love....

I bet you're wondering how you can meet everyone else.

Star Lake Series:

Sealed with a Kiss: Meet the quirky cast of Star Lake and find out if Max and Layla will ever find love.

When Love Returns: Return to Star Lake to hear Presley's story and find out if she gets the second chance with her first love.

Once Upon a Star: Continue the journey when aspiring actress Audrey returns home with a baby. Will Blake finally get the nerve to share his feelings with her?

Love Conquers All: Meet Lanie Perkins Hall who never imagined being divorced at thirty or falling for an old friend, but will his secrets keep them apart?

The Star Lake Collection: Get the latter three stories in one place. Series will include book 1 when it releases around November 2020.

The Heartbeats Series:

Where It All Began: Sandra Baker finds forgiveness and healing even after making a horrible choice.

The Power of Prayer: Will Callie Green find true love or be defined by her mistake?

When Hearts Collide: When Amanda Adams goes to college, she finds a world she was not ready for. But will she also find true love?

A Past Forgiven: Jess Peterson has lived a life of abuse and lost her self worth, but when she finds herself pregnant, will she find new hope?

The Heartbeats Collection: Grab all four Heartbeats novels in one collection

Sweet Billionaires Series:

The Billionaire's Impromptu Bet: Can a spoiled rich girl change when a bet turns to love?

The Billionaire's Secret: Can a playboy settle down when he finds out he has a daughter who needs him?

A Brush with a Billionaire: What happens when a stuck up actor lands in a small town and needs help from a female mechanic?

The Billionaire's Christmas Miracle: A twist on a Cinderella story when a billionaire meets a woman who doesn't belong at the ball.

The Billionaire's Cowboy Groom: Will one night six years ago keep Carrie from finding true love?

The Cowboy Billionaire: Coming Soon!

The Billionaire's Bliss: This collection contains The Billionaire's Secret, The Billionaire's Christmas Miracle, and The Billionaire's Cowboy Groom

The Lawkeeper Series:

Lawfully Matched: When the man she agreed to marry turns out to have a dark past, will Kate have to return home or will she find love with her rescuer in this historical fiction?

Lawfully Justified: Can a bounty hunter and a widow find love together in this historical fiction?

The Scarlet Wedding: William and Emma are planning their wedding, but an outbreak and a return from his past force them to change their plans. Is a happily ever after still in their future in this historical fiction?

Lawfully Redeemed: What happens when a K9 cop falls for the brother of her suspect? Contemporary romance.

The Lawkeeper Collection: Get all four books in one collection

The Are You Listening Series:

The Still Small Voice: Will Jordan listen to God's prompting in this speculative fiction?

A Spark in the Darkness Will Jordan be able to help Raven before the rapture occurs?

Blushing Brides Series:

The Cowboy's Reality Bride: He's agreed to be the bachelor on a reality dating show, but what happens when he falls for a woman who's not one of the contestants?

The Reality Bride's Baby: Laney wants nothing more than a baby, but when she starts feeling dizzy is it pregnancy or something more serious?

The Producer's Unlikely Bride: What happens when a producer and an author agree to a fake relationship?

Ava's Blessing in Disguise: Five years after marriage, Ava faces a mysterious illness that threatens to ruin her career. Will she find out what it is?

The Soldier's Steadfast Bride: coming soon

The Men of Fire Beach

Fire Games: Cassidy returns home from Who Wants to Marry a Cowboy to find obsessive letters from a fan. The cop assigned to help her wants to get back to his case, but what she sees at a fire may just be the key he's looking for.

Lost Memories and New Beginnings: A doctor, a patient with no memory, the men out to get her. Can he keep her safe when he doesn't know who he's looking for?

When Questions Abound: A Companion story to Lost Memories. Told from Detective Graves' point of view.

Never Forget the Past: Fireman Bubba must confront his past in order to clear his name and save lives.

Love on the Run: Graham is forced into lockdown

with one of his employees. Will he be able to save her from her ex and will she steal his heart?

Secrets and Suspense: Cara Hunter is hiding something about her military past. When she's suspected of murder, will she be able to convince Cole she's the victim?

Rescue My Heart: Al's sister has gone missing. Can she save her? And who is the man she meets? Friend or foe?

The Men of Fire Beach Collection: Books 1-3

Texas Tornadoes

Defending My Heart: Forced to confront his past, Emmitt finds news that will change his life.

Run With My Heart: Sentenced to community service, Tucker finds himself falling for the manager.

Love on the Line: Blaine has hired Kenzi to redo his cabin, but what happens when she finds his darkest secret?

Touchdown on Love: When Mason's injury throws him together with ex-girlfriend, will sparks fly again?

Second Chance Reception: Jefferson is hiding something. When he falls for the team cook, will he let her in?

Small Town Short Stories

Small Town Dreams

Small Town Second Chances

Small Town Rivals

Small Town Life

Life in a Small Town: All four stories in one collection

Stand Alones:

Love Renewed: This books is part of the multi author second chance series. When fate reunites high school sweethearts separated by life's choices, can they find a second chance at love at a snowy lodge amid a little mystery?

Her children's early reader chapter book series:

The Wishing Stone #1: Dangerous Dinosaur

The Wishing Stone #2: Dragon Dilemma

The Wishing Stone #3: Mesmerizing Mermaids

The Wishing Stone #4: Pyramid Puzzle

The Wishing Stone: Mary's Miracle

The Wishing Stone Collection

To see a list of all her books

authorloranahoopes.com

loranahoopes@gmail.com

ABOUT THE AUTHOR

Lorana Hoopes is an inspirational author originally from Texas but now living in the PNW with her husband and three children. When not writing, she can be seen kick-boxing at the gym, singing, or acting on stage. One day, she hopes to retire from teaching and write full time.

www.ingramcontent.com/pod-product-compliance
Lightning Source LLC
Chambersburg PA
CBHW030307200626

46816CB00002BA/797